THE WILL OF THE TRIBE

Mysteries by Arthur W. Upfield
available as Scribner Crime Classics:

DEATH OF A LAKE
DEATH OF A SWAGMAN
THE DEVIL'S STEPS
MURDER DOWN UNDER
THE NEW SHOE
SINISTER STONES

THE WILL OF THE TRIBE

Arthur W. Upfield

CHARLES SCRIBNER'S SONS
NEW YORK

CONTENTS

THE WILL OF THE TRIBE

1

LUCIFER'S COUCH

Inspector Napoleon Bonaparte gazed upon Lucifer's Couch and marvelled.

The Stranger must have been of considerable size to have made such a mark on this land of lemon-tinted sand and red-gold rock. He arrived, it is recalled by people who lived at Hall's Creek, late in December, 1905, to dig a pit several hundred feet deep and one mile in circumference, and to raise about it a rampart of rock and rubble some hundred feet above the surrounding plain. Such was the impact, the shock upthrust three observable rings of rock-rubble: the inner half a mile from the pit, the middle about three quarters of a mile, and the outer a full mile from the centre.

It was no glancing blow but a direct fall, for the wall about the pit is perfectly circular and, save at one place, uniform in height and width at the summit. The occasional heavy monsoon rain and the high winds of spring and autumn have removed from the rubble the earth which originally cemented the hard micaceous sandstone forming the wall, producing a polished monument as conceived by a Pharaoh's architect and built by a Pharaoh's slave labour. Inside the wall the earth and sand of the floor of the pit now slopes gently to the central soak-hole about which grow several desert hardwoods.

"A hundred feet above the plain, Howard, and from two

to three hundred feet down to that soak," observed Inspector Bonaparte. "Give me the history."

First Constable Howard, tough and seemingly as polished by the sun and the wind as the wall on which they were sitting, complied:

"The meteor fell in 1905, and the people who saw it fall won't take it from a couple of geologists that it fell three hundred years ago. The people at Hall's Creek watched the flaming mass and heard the detonation. They were only sixty-five miles distant.

"In those days this country wasn't taken up by cattlemen, the outlet for Hall's Creek being at Wyndham on the north coast. No one travelled down this way to investigate. When Beaudesert was taken up, their stockmen never troubled to climb up here, for, from any point, the place looks like a low flat-topped stony hill. This crater was actually discovered as late as 1947 by a party of oil prospectors who happened to fly over it.

"Following the discovery," Howard proceeded, "barely a dozen stockmen came here, and in 1948 members of an expedition sent by the Australian Geographic Society photographed and reported on it. Later, another party came, following the truck tracks of the first.

"Now we come to the present year, April 27, and again a plane chanced to fly over and the people aboard saw in the pit what they thought was a body. It was a body right enough. White man, dead several days. How he had got there, who he was, no one could tell. He was without swag, water bag, any equipment. His clothes were soiled and damaged, and his boots needed repair.

"You know, of course, that no one gets around in this country without being reported on the radio network. No matter if he's a touring politician or a prospector, a stranger is news, an item of gossip for all the station homesteads to talk about. We're three hundred miles from

Derby on the west; Wyndham on the north is two hundred miles, and it's something like five hundred miles from Darwin. Inside those points there are many homesteads and more aboriginal tribes, and no one, black or white, ever reported the dead man."

"The nearer homesteads, Deep Creek and Beaudesert," suggested Bonaparte. "People at one or the other could have been concerned with the death of this man."

"Must have been," agreed the policeman. "But these homesteads are both comparatively close, and no stranger could have got to them without being reported having passed through homesteads beyond them. You can see Deep Creek Homestead. The track down from the Hall's Creek-Derby through Beaudesert road doesn't go beyond. Beyond is desert for a thousand miles and more, and in this desert are a hundred per cent wild abos. We haven't been able to track the dead man from any point, let alone identify him. The only theory which isn't a theory is that he fell from a plane, but he didn't because nothing is broken bar his skull."

Bonaparte stood to gaze over the surrounding desert, facing north. He could see the inner and middle rock rings and the demarkation of the limit of country burned to ash by the heat of the Stranger. Beyond that line the scrub trees were older, and beyond them grew the ancient gums bordering Deep Creek. The Creek trees appeared to be the hem of the multi-coloured rug of the Kimberley Ranges with their flat-capped red residuals, razor-edged green escarpments, and deep black gullies.

Three miles to the west could be seen the homestead of Deep Creek cattle station, and even casual examination of a map would show the officially named Wolf Creek Meteor Crater to be situated at the northern edge of the great inland desert of Western Australia.

"The trees on the plain aren't any older than those down

at the soakage," Constable Howard was saying. "Proving, I'd say that the meteor fell less than sixty years ago, not three hundred."

To the east as well as toward the west, the mountains rested upon the flat base of the desert, at this time of day looking darkly forbidding to the airy brilliance of the plain stretching southward beyond the edge of the world. Bonaparte sat again and worked on another cigarette. He said: "Bring the history of this place up to date, continuing as from the discovery of the body down there. I've read the Case Summary but I'd like to hear it from you."

"The body was seen by members of the Mineral Survey party on April 27. Early this day the manager of Deep Creek and his stockmen left on a muster down south. At the homestead, normal routine work went on. Lubras doing the household wash, an aborigine called Captain breaking in a horse, the manager's wife doing her usual chores, and their two little girls being given their lessons by an educated aboriginal lass called Tessa.

"The plane party dropped a note shortly after ten that morning. The note said: 'Believe there is a man hurt or dead in the Crater. Think you should investigate.' The homestead cook, a white man named Jim Scolloti, and the abo called Captain came here in the cook's old utility." Howard pointed out the clearly defined track winding from the Crater toward the distant homestead. "That track was first made by the cook's utility and then used by the traffic during the subsequent investigation.

"Now when the two of them got back to the homestead, Mrs. Brentner, the manager's wife, tried to work the transceiver. Neither she nor the cook knew much about it, and they couldn't get it to work. So Scolloti drove the twenty-seven miles to Beaudesert, where they raised Base, and Base contacted me. I left at once, arriving at the homestead pretty late as the track . . . but you know the track we came over today.

"When I got to Beaudesert with my two trackers, Mrs. Leroy said her husband had the Deep Creek transceiver working, and had told her that all the blacks had cleared out on walkabout after hearing about the body down there. Even the breaker, Captain, and the young lubra called Tessa, cleared out too. But they had come back when I got to Deep Creek.

"It was then close to dark, and I wasn't going to muck up tracks about this place by wandering around in the night. Soon after break of day, with Leroy and the trackers, I came here and we all went down to the body. The tracks made by the cook and the abo horse-breaker were clear enough, but even my trackers couldn't locate the tracks of any other person, not even the tracks of the dead man. If the dead man walked to where his body was found he must have left his tracks. If he was carried there, the man or men who carried him must have left tracks. But, as I said, the only tracks down there were those made by the cook and the abo. I had the trackers skirt the entire outside of the wall, and they couldn't pick up tracks. And both of them are good too."

Constable Howard interrupted his narrative to light a cigarette, and proceeded. "My junior got here with Doctor Reedy in the afternoon. Doc Reedy examined the body. It was badly mauled by the birds, but he's stuck to his opinion made at the time that the feller had been dead three days at shortest, and six at longest. Due to the complete absence of humidity, parts of the body not attacked by the birds told Doc the man had once had smallpox, and, as one hand has been protected, we managed to obtain a clear set of prints. Also we took the set of dentures. Age of man about forty-five. Height five feet eleven. Boot size eight. Hat size seven and three quarters. Weight about twelve stone. Clothes similar to those worn by the average bushman.

"The Inspector and the Derby doctor arrived the next day, and the two doctors agreed on Doc Reedy's first opinion. There wasn't anything more to do with the body save take it to Hall's Creek and have it buried. The Coroner found that the man had been murdered by a blunt instrument applied to the back of the skull with considerable force."

"Let's go down to the place marked X," decided Bonaparte.

As they descended, as the wall of the rim heightened above them, the immensity of this crater became more and more impressive, and when standing on the sandy loam of the floor it was found easy to visualise what the rising tiers of an arena must have appeared to the anguished eyes of the victims of the Roman Games. The sun gilded the vast rampart of rocks. The slight wind outside didn't penetrate. The temperature was at least ten degrees higher, and on a summer day might well be fifty degrees hotter. Howard led the way to the spot still marked by four wood pegs.

"It was lying on its back," he said. "One arm out from the shoulder, the other doubled under the buttocks. The legs were straight but raised slightly at the knees. The doctors thought it possible that rigor mortis had set in when the body was dumped. They were positive it was dumped. Otherwise carried here."

"And no tracks, inside or outside the Crater, you said."

"Not a skerrick of a track."

"The aborigines are past masters at erasing tracks, and very good indeed in avoiding leaving tracks," Bonaparte said, unnecessarily, while standing at the edge of the soak-hole partially masked by several desert scrub trees. It was fifteen feet across and about eight feet deep, and there were the bones of more than one kangaroo that had been bogged in the mud. Now it was hard.

"The body was first seen on April 27," Bony remarked. "It is now August 7. Roughly fourteen weeks. The tracks down here are well preserved by the encircling wall. When was the search for evidence abandoned?"

"On the eighteenth of May," replied Howard. "It was a sort of grand final. Brentner and his men returned with cattle on May 12, and they joined with the trackers and Captain and the Deep Creek blacks who came from walk-about a couple of days before. We almost tore the ruddy wall down that day."

They climbed the wall, often having to use their hands so steep was it, and again relaxed on the summit.

"Did your trackers say what they thought of the affair?" asked Bonaparte.

"No. I got the idea that they were uneasy about it all. But then the blacks are always uneasy over anything they don't understand."

"What's your opinion? A black or a white killing?"

"I couldn't vote for one or the other. I'll vote for the blacks being concerned somewhere along the line. There's two sections of aborigines: the wild blokes down south and the semi-civilised fellers like these at Deep Creek and at Beaudesert. I'm not a Kimberleys man like the sergeant at Wyndham. He reckons it was wild blacks who did the killing and that the tame blacks would just go dumb about it."

"And they can be dumb, too, Howard. We may leave it that way, and get along to Deep Creek. The Brentners are said to be sociable people. I may have to test it for a month and more. What's Brentner's history?"

"Came up the rough way. According to the Wyndham sergeant, Brentner started as a stockman, then became a drover, and then owned his own drover's outfit. Had all the north of Australia to play around in. He never concerned us, and always seemed to co-operate. In a civil action now and then over cattle being mixed up: his employers and other owners. That sort of thing. Then he got the job managing Deep Creek, and he went down to Perth and married a big businessman's secretary. They chortled when he brought her up here, but they don't chortle now. Marriage fixed Kurt Brentner. It fixes most of us, I'd say."

"It does have a calming influence," Bonaparte said, laughing. "I believe I shall have a pleasant time here. Almost a holiday. A little anthropological work to maintain interest in spare moments. In the report to your Inspector tell him that. Inspectors love to be told something or other. It calms them, don't you think?"

"Take an axe to calm my Inspector." Then Howard remembered and added: "Sorry, I forgot you're a bit above a constable, sir."

"Well, keep on forgetting it. And the sir. Any questions?"

"I'd like to ask one. I've had the feeling that the murder of this unknown man was a little outside the ordinary. Now after all these weeks, you are assigned to it. Is he important?"

"To a few people he is most important. I stress the present tense. It's why I'm here."

2

THE BRENTNERS

The homestead was built on a slight rise southward of Deep Creek by some five hundred yards. It was a commodious building of variegated materials, having been begun as a four-room cottage and now comprising a dozen rooms under the one roof extending over the twelve-feet-wide verandahs. Detached from the main building were the kitchen and the usual day-house constructed with buffalo grass, both being connected by a covered way with the house. A wire-netted fence created about these buildings a roomy compound where grew bean trees and several flowering gums.

The trade shops, the store, and the men's quarters, the horse- and cattle-yards, and the motor shed were situated to the west of the compound, and were dominated by reservoir water tanks on high platforms.

On the east verandah this afternoon of August 7 were Rose Brentner and her two children, Rosie and Hilda, with Tessa who had been adopted by the Brentners. All were dressed in white, and each was a component of a perfect tropical picture in the cool and dry season of winter.

Rose Brentner was in her early thirties, athletic still, inclined to leanness. Her hair was brown with golden tints. Her eyes were brown and apt to open wide when intensely interested. She was a tall woman, and, when she spoke, her voice betrayed the preciseness of business training.

Rosie, aged seven, had her colouring. Hilda was like her father, fair, with hazel eyes having the innocence of a baby of two, and she five years old.

"I wish Mr. Howard and Inspector Bonaparte would come," Rosie said with some impatience. "When people are coming they ought to come at once. Is the Inspector the son of the Emperor of France?"

"I don't think so," replied her mother. "I hope not. We're not prepared to receive Royalty. Try to remember your dates."

"Captain said that Mr. Howard and Inspector Bonaparte drove to Lucifer's Couch before lunch. He saw their dust," volunteered Hilda who was standing at the verandah screen. "I can see dust too."

The elder child ran to join her and a moment later agreed that Constable Howard's jeep was approaching. The aboriginal girl joined the children. Not beautiful, she was pleasing to look at now she was seventeen years old and at her best. Civilisation in the persons of the Brentners had given her body robustness and poise to stand with the children without conscious inferiority. Her voice was soft and without accent. Little Hilda took her hand excitedly and pointed at the rising brown dust gilded by the sun.

"It will be they," Tessa said. "They're on the track from the Crater. Look! There's Captain on the tank stand, and he's signalling too. Shall I call Kurt?"

"Yes, do, Tessa," assented Rose. "We'll have afternoon tea in the day-house. Will you see to it?"

Tessa hurried into the house, and Rose Brentner, with the girls, left to cross the compound to the gate fronting the Creek. There her husband joined them, a large man, rugged and tough, fair hair already thinning, hazel eyes made small by the sun. Like the men who alighted from the jeep, he wore khaki drill slacks and open-neck shirt.

No one appeared to notice the distant semi-circle of aborigines beyond the jeep or the aborigine who had been on the tank stand and now was waving to the crowd to stand clear. Rose and her husband smiled at Howard, and swiftly focussed attention on the second man advancing to them with smiling blue eyes.

Howard said: "Inspector Bonaparte. Mr. Brentner and Mrs. Brentner."

Rose Brentner received slight shock. She had heard of this man, and he wasn't anything like the mental build-up she had done when hearing he was coming. The only trace of his aboriginal ancestry was his colouring, a shade darker than that of her husband's weathered features. He appeared slight as he shook hands with the cattleman, but then most men did so when near him. Then he was bending over her proffered hand and smiling.

"You must be sick and tired of policemen, Mrs. Brentner. I shall try hard not to be a nuisance."

"You are very welcome, Inspector," Rose heard herself say. "People like us naturally welcome everyone." She glanced at her small daughters. "We have been a little impatient too."

"Ah!" Bonaparte bent low to greet the girls. "You'll be Rosie, and you will be Hilda. How d'you do! Mrs. Leroy was telling me of you, and she sent her love to you."

"Mrs. Leroy spoils both of 'em," interjected Brentner.

"I find that hard to believe," countered Bonaparte. "No one could ever spoil these young ladies. Mrs. Leroy told me they both know beautiful aboriginal legends, and I hope to hear them sometime."

"You will," Brentner said positively. "Did I see Tessa with afternoon tea?"

The visitors could not have been more warmly welcomed had they been close relatives. They were conducted to the day-house which offered surprises by its roominess and furnishing. It was circular in shape and contained easy chairs, racks of books, a large dining table, and several floor rugs. The young aborigine turned from setting out the tea things, and her large black eyes slowly found Bonaparte after smiling at Constable Howard.

"So you are Tessa! I am happy to meet you, Tessa."

"You are very kind, Inspector. How do you do!"

"Well, now we're all here and comfortable, what about a cup of tea?" suggested Brentner, winking at Hilda. "Our friends must be as famished as I am, what with all the work I've done today."

"You've done nothing all day but read the pastoral journals," accused his wife, and Brentner grinned and wanted to know if Inspector Bonaparte was married.

Tessa poured the tea, and the children gravely conveyed it to the guests and their parents.

"Would you all grant a favor?" Bonaparte asked, and waited for their assurance. "Actually it's two favors. The first is that you try to forget I am a policeman. You could never forget that Constable Howard is one because he cannot help looking like one. The second favor is that you call me Bony. My wife does. My three sons do. I hope I can persuade you. I did persuade Mrs. Leroy."

A small hand was rested on his knee, and Hilda said: "Can we call you Bony, too, Inspector Bonaparte?"

"Of course. Inspector Bonaparte is a bit of mouthful, isn't it?"

Hilda gravely nodded agreement and joined her sister.

It was Kurt Brentner who suggested that the visitors might like to talk business and that his office would be relaxing. Bony expressed the hope that Mrs. Brentner would join them later.

The office also provided a surprise, being a commodious room having two pairs of french windows. The radio transceiver, black panelled with chrome fittings, first captured the attention. Other than the roll-top American desk, flanked by steel cabinets, there was nothing of the office about this comfortably furnished apartment. Brentner invited his guests to sit and smoke, and, having remarked that some cattlemen appeared to be most fortunate, Bony crossed to the french windows to gaze out over the desert to the gold brick lying on the horizon.

"Mrs. Leroy told us Mrs. Brentner named it Lucifer's Couch," he said. "So much more picturesque than the official Wolf Creek Meteor Crater. D'you mind if I close the windows?"

"Not at all. Chilly?"

"No. The verandah could be accommodating." Having closed both pairs of windows, Bony accepted the easy chair drawn to the low occasional table on which were cigarettes and tobacco. He was smiling when he said: "Cops and robbers, you know. Nasty suspicious policemen."

"Stock in trade," Brentner said good-humouredly.

"We were trained to be suspicious," Bony said, laughing softly. "Before Mrs. Brentner joins us, I would like to know something of this local scene and the people. I've glanced at the Police Summary of the crime at the Crater, but only glanced. I understand you have been in this part of the Continent all your life. You would be au fait with the aborigines, meaning as knowledgeable as most. Is there a legend about Lucifer's Couch?"

"I haven't heard of one," replied Brentner. "Our Tessa could answer. She's interested in legends."

"I must ask her. By the way, do please treat our subject confidentially. We must start on the premise that the man found in the Crater could not possibly have got there without the knowledge of the aborigines. I refer to the aborigines here at Deep Creek, those at Beaudesert, the tribes either side of them, and the wild blacks down south on the desert. Do you agree?"

"Yes. But . . ."

"Pardon me. At this stage my mind is open. The murder could have been committed by the local aborigines, the wild ones, or whites in this wide area. What I desire to pin down is this. The dead man could not have been put in the Crater without the knowledge of the aborigines, and further, he could not, in the first instance, have entered this area of the Kimberleys in the North and Desert in the South without it being a news item to all the tribes and sections. Do you agree?"

"As you put it, yes."

"Then we have three suppositions. One that the murder was done by the whites. Two that it was done by the blacks. And three that it was committed by the whites and the blacks in collusion. Thus: white, black, black-white. Pity we cannot add yellow. I like my investigations most involved."

"You have an involved one here," Howard dryly observed.

"Mrs. Leroy thinks that your aborigines are allied with those at Beaudesert who are Kimberley blacks. How do your aborigines get along with the wild men?"

"There's been no real trouble for many years. The tribal grounds belonging to our people extend to about forty miles to the south, and includes the Crater."

"Tell me, do you think your aborigines are as assimilated with the whites as much as, say, the Beaudesert tribe?"

Brentner was positive when he answered in the negative.

"Forgive me for being boring. Can you say to whom your people are closer . . . the wild blacks or the Beaudesert blacks?"

"It's hard to be sure about that. I'd say they were nearer to the desert blacks. And you're not being boring."

"Thank you. Tell me about Tessa, how you came to adopt her."

"Well, my wife and I were sitting in the day-house one evening, nine years ago, when a child ran in and threw herself at my wife's feet, hugged her legs, and begged to stay with us. She was to be married the next day, tribal fashion, to an abo old enough to be her grandfather. The wife said I'd have to stop it. She was new up here and didn't understand the problem. Not nearly like the kid did, and I did, too.

"Anyway, Rose took her off to the bathroom, scrubbed her down, put her in her own bed, locked the door, and left me sitting up expecting trouble. Trouble didn't come, and early the next morning, Rose still determined, I went to the camp and yabbered to Chief Gup-Gup and Poppa the Medicine Man. The upshot was I bought the kid for a few plugs of tobacco, and finally we adopted her. She's turned out well, as no doubt you noticed."

"I agree. How close is she to her people?"

"Goes along now and then to visit her mother and the others. That's all. Lives with us, of course. She's one of the family. Calls me Kurt and the wife Rose. Rose educated her to the point that we had ambition to send her down to a Teachers College. She's teaching our kids now. She turned out well, and we are both proud of our Tessa. Shows what can be done if you get 'em early, and get 'em away from their elders."

"I think it shows, rather, what love can do. What of the man called Captain?"

"My own kids called him that," Brentner explained. "Leroy managed the place before me, and he was married to a Salvation Army lass in Broome. You met her, of course. Tragedy she went blind. Anyway, she got the abo children together and tried to give them something of Christianity. The lad we call Captain was fast at picking up ideas, but

I think Mrs. Leroy didn't do much with the rest. She sent him to the Padre at Derby who put him to school, and he got along real well until fifteen. Then he did what we all expected. He just turned up. Get him serious and he'll talk better than me. His handwriting is something to admire. But, well, you know how it is."

"Please dig deeper."

"When he came back he was a real mixed-up kid, as they say," proceeded the cattleman. "We'd been here only a few months, and Rose tried hard to get him to continue his schooling under her. But no. He couldn't be assimilated like our Tessa. It was too late. He belonged to the camp, and, being the son of Gup-Gup's son, I've always thought they influenced him. But they didn't get him back a hundred per cent.

"He got to like being with the cook, looking after the chooks, doing odd jobs without being asked. A few years after he came back from Derby I found him asleep in the saddlery shop, and he'd gone to sleep reading a book. We had a quiet talk, and the upshot of that was I let him have an out-house to himself. Rose got him books to read, and eventually he became a sort of overseer with the blacks. I want stockmen; he singles them out. He breaks in the horses. Comes running if Rose whistles. Eats most times with the cook. Plays tracking with my kids and tells 'em abo legends. And is a damned good go-between with the Tribe."

"How old, d'you think?"

"About twenty-five."

"A lubra?"

"Never took one that we know of."

"Now for the cook. His name is . . ." Bony stopped and rose when Mrs. Brentner entered: "Welcome to our little conference."

3

THE HONOURED GUEST

Rose Brentner's business training had sharpened her perception of trifles, and she didn't fail to note that Bony had conducted her to a chair to sit with her back to the strong light and that he faced the light. She wondered if this was due to purpose or to vanity. She noted, too, that his easy manner when in the day-house was replaced by restrained assertiveness, giving him command of this conference which her husband and Constable Howard had already acknowledged. She had expected brashness, flamboyancy, and in the day-house she had met charm and ease. Now she felt strength and the poise given by experience.

As her husband told of their cook, Jim Scolloti, of his long service and his dependability so long as he did not smell alcohol, she noted that Bony was missing nothing although his blue eyes were almost lazily directed beyond the windows.

"You have two white stockmen," pressed Bony.

"Just the two," replied the cattleman. "As the kids named Captain, they have named them Old Ted and Young Col. You'll meet them at dinner. Old Ted is twenty-six, and Young Col is twenty. Both are a cut above the old-time bush rider, being college educated. Old Ted has money of his own, having inherited from his parents who were killed in a road accident. Young Col's father owns farming properties down in the Riverina, wants him to manage one, but, like Old Ted, he won't leave these parts. Col's been with us four years; Old Ted seven."

"And you have been here ten years, I understand, having taken over from Mr. Leroy who established the station eighteen years ago. There are your two white stockmen, your cook, and yourself: four white men. Can you tell me just what your men did during six days prior to the discovery of the dead man in the Crater?"

Brentner made as though to get up, and was waved back.

"Wait, please. Be patient. The medical opinion is that the man was dead from three to six days. He was found three miles from this homestead, on the Deep Creek Pastoral Property, and in this part of Australia three miles is reckoned as being just outside the back door."

Brentner took from one of the steel cabinets a normal business diary. Flicking open the pages, his fingers betrayed impatience, and, on speaking, he tried without success to control his voice.

"You want six days of work, Inspector. Well, here they are beginning at April 21. That day Old Ted and four black stockmen from the local tribe were droving a mob of cattle to Beaudesert to be handed to a drover taking them to Derby. Young Col and one black stockman were looking over the grass country at Eddy's Well. They were camped there. On this day, with Rose and the kids, I left at ten o'clock for Hall's Creek.

"On April 22 we came back as far as Beaudesert where we stayed the night. Old Ted arrived there with the cattle, and Young Col was still at Eddy's Well. On the twenty-third we got home about eleven in the morning and Old Ted returned from Beaudesert about four. Young Col was still away at Eddy's. He returned the next day, the twenty-fourth, and this day I worked here in the office and Old

Ted repaired saddlery. We had a spell on the twenty-fifth. On the twenty-sixth we prepared to leave for the muster, and on the twenty-seventh we left at seven in the morning. It was this day that the plane people saw the body. Enough?"

"During the period was there any unrest, any trouble with your aborigines?"

"They were quiet as usual," replied Brentner, sitting down again.

"Thank you. Now I'll state my own position. I've been seconded by my Department to an instrumentality of the Federal Government to find answers to two questions. One question is how did the man found dead in the Crater penetrate this far into the Kimberley Region without having been reported by the station homesteads, and the other is what was he doing prior to his death? It is known who he was, and thus the answers to these questions are important to the Federal Instrumentality, which is not interested particularly in how he met his death."

"Oh!" softly exclaimed Rose Brentner. "Who was he, then?"

"It was the question I asked, and I was not informed, it being thought extraneous to the purpose of my investigation. However, the Western Australian Police Department sought and was granted my seconding to investigate the killing of this, even to me, unknown man. It would appear that I am to serve two masters."

Rose Brentner watched the long brown fingers rolling a cigarette, and then she studied the dark brown face on which aboriginal race moulding was absent. The face was neither round nor long. The nose was straight, the mouth flexible. The brows were not unlike a verandah to shadow the unusual blue eyes, and although the black hair was now greying at the temples, it was virile and well kept.

Then he was looking at her, and the features vanished before the power of the eyes.

"It is agreed, I believe, that anyone travelling through the Kimberleys is reported when arriving at or passing through a station over the radio network. Such a person is news for everyone here, and because of the great distances between the station homesteads, the constantly known whereabouts of the traveller is almost vital for his own safety."

Bony now took Brentner into his confidence, and Howard leaned forward as though he thought he might miss something.

"Without doubt you are familiar with the geography of this north-west corner of Australia, but I will use the simile of the open fan to illustrate the circumstances about this case. We will place the handle of the opened fan at Lucifer's Couch. Out along the left vane, or whatever it is, lie half a dozen homesteads on the track to Derby. Out along the centre are half a dozen homesteads, including the town of Hall's Creek, on the track to Wyndham. And along the right vane other homesteads lie on the track to Darwin. The traveller enters these Kimberleys by one of those tracks, as there is no other. It is my opinion that the traveller could come here only across the desert to the south, from a point on its perimeter a thousand-odd miles away.

"He couldn't cross that desert without the wild aborigines knowing all about him, any more than a traveller can cross the Kimberleys without the station aborigines knowing all about his movements. You, Mr. Brentner, and Constable Howard, will surely agree with me that the aborigines still removed from long and close association with the whites also have a broadcasting system developed through past centuries, and I think you will agree with me, too, that espionage organisations set up by outside governments are amateurish by comparison with the methods employed by these Australian aborigines who could make the cloak-and-dagger boys stand gaping at street corners.

"Forgive me for being repetitious. I shall be asking for your co-operation, and should be grateful did I receive it. Your own aborigines know who killed that man and who put him in the Crater. They might not have had anything to do with the crime, but their elders surely know the details. Thus we proceed without taking into our confidence any aborigine, including Captain and Tessa. Will you think about it?"

Rose Brentner smiled and stood, saying: "Of course, Bony. Just look at the time! Dinner will be ready in an hour, and I've to dress. Can we continue afterwards?"

"I may have to test your hospitality for several weeks, and we must not permit ourselves to be bored by any one subject."

Bony was assured that no subject could be boring to people starved for outside contacts, and was conducted to a pleasant room facing across the compound to the creek trees. Having been given the hint by Howard, he changed into more formal clothes and, on hearing a triangle beaten with a bar, made his way to the dining room. Here he found his host and Howard with two young men gathered before a sideboard, and was offered beer or sherry.

A red-bearded, blue-eyed man was presented to him as Old Ted, and a boy looking no older than sixteen was presented as Young Col. Young Col's hair was fair and over-long, and his hazel eyes glinted with mischief. Both spoke with a polished accent.

"We have heard about you, Inspector," Young Col said, raising his glass as though to toast. "Nothing to your discredit. Could I be wrong, Ted?"

"Not this time," replied the bearded man, and raising

his glass, added: "Here's to the guest of honour. May his stay with us always be peaceful."

"It always will, provided you call me Bony."

"Delighted. What d'you reckon, Chief?" inquired the red-bearded man.

"Comes easy to the tongue," agreed the cattleman.

Tessa appeared, this time with the two children. Bony greeted them and smiled into their excited eyes. A tall thin man in chef's livery appeared carrying a large platter and was followed by a young aborigine woman, wearing cap and apron over a black dress, bearing another tray.

The room, the appointments, the company, Bony found most pleasing, and quickly realised it was due to Rose Brentner's long influence over this homestead. Her husband talked easily; the young men teased Howard; the children asked questions without seeming to intrude; and Tessa supervised their meal. He was promised introduction to a Mister Lamb who was a pet sheep, to a Mrs. Bluey, the mother of a litter of five pups, and to a pet kangaroo called Bob Menzies.

He met Mister Lamb the following morning when arranging with Howard about times he could be contacted by radio, and, having watched the policeman's jeep disappear beyond the creek crossing, he was made aware of this animal by being bunted gently against his leg. Little Hilda then informed him that Mister Lamb requested a cigarette, and she was enumerating Mister Lamb's virtues and vices when she was called to the schoolroom by her mother.

Rose beckoned, and Bony joined her on the verandah. She said: "Come along in for morning tea. I'm dying to gossip, and I want to know all about you. The men will be busy all morning, so I have my chance."

"Everyone knows all about me," he told her, lightly.

"I don't. I'm an inquisitive woman. To us you are wonderfully unusual."

"I am the most unusual man in Australia," was the humourously expressed claim. He was laughing, and she knew it was at himself. As he told her of his origins and the highlights of his career, victories over himself rather than of others, the sense of superiority which had been with her was expunged from her mind. She admitted she hadn't been able to brew tea in a billycan when she came to Deep Creek as a bride, and she spoke of the many amenities she had missed and the blessing she had been given. Eventually he asked if he might talk shop, and to this she nodded.

"I'd like to go into your experiences on that day the plane people dropped the message," he said. "It was a bad day, wasn't it?"

"Everything went wrong from the moment I read the message."

"So I'm given to understand. You couldn't get the transceiver working, and yet Mr. Leroy found no difficulty in opening up. There is the possibility that someone disconnected something to delay word getting to Howard and then made the connection just before Leroy got here. What do you think?"

"It was talked about, I know. But who would do that? No, what happened, I believe, is that Jim and I were so excited we couldn't do the right things to make it work. Neither of us know much about it."

"What of Captain and Tessa?" Bony pressed.

"You may count them out. They don't know the first thing about it."

"Well, whatever the cause, the delay occasioned by Scolloti having to go to Beaudesert to contact Howard measured almost one day. That one day might have been important. I don't know."

"But why should anyone have interfered with the transceiver?"

Bony shrugged faintly, saying: "Life would be easy if we had the answers to all the questions. When you and Scolloti went outside again everyone had vanished, save the children. Even Tessa had disappeared, and it wasn't till after sundown that Tessa returned with Captain, or rather Captain came home bringing Tessa with him. Tessa had been crying, and her dress was torn as though she had been forcibly brought home. The explanation given Howard was that the Tribe had suddenly decided on a walkabout, which is quite normal, and that Tessa and Captain went off with the Tribe. Again quite normal, both being members of it. Tell me, what was Tessa's explanation to you?"

"That she ran away with the others and thought better of it after Captain made her come back."

"Please!" The blue eyes had caught her, and she couldn't evade them. "Nine years ago a child sought your protection. She was never initiated; she was adopted by you. Today she is almost fully assimilated. Her dress sense is excellent. Her poise very good. Her conversation is intelligent and lucid. And she would just run off with the Tribe when told? Her explanation, please."

"Well, it wasn't exactly like that. When I taxed her about it, she wouldn't say anything. Then she said she didn't know why. Eventually she confessed that the lubras beckoned and she had felt something inside compelling her to run after them. I wonder! Kurt thinks it was the collective will of the Tribe. Can you agree with that?"

"Certainly. But what prompted the will of the Tribe to command your Tessa. You and the children were left utterly alone after the cook went off to report. You and the children went to the camp and found it completely deserted. On your return you cleaned your husband's guns and decided to sleep in the store-room as it seemed the strongest place. And then in the early evening Captain returned with Tessa, and the girl crying and her dress torn. The picture is clear enough, but there's something wrong with it."

4

OBJECTS OF GOLD

In contradistinction to the Interior aborigines, the Kimberley natives are well built, tall, graceful in walk and poise. It has been considered likely that these people were the last to migrate from the northern islands, then driving the original inhabitants into the inhospitable arid lands, as the original inhabitants of the continent had been driven down into Tasmania before that island was separated from the mainland.

Captain was a typical Kimberleys man. He was five feet ten in height; he was well formed and in excellent physical condition, partly due to the fare provided by Jim Scolloti. The cutting scars either side of his backbone went far to prove his complete initiation, and the absence of cuts on his chest proved that he hadn't risen to a place among the elite of his Tribe.

Bony watched him at work on a young gelding. Man and horse were within a circular yard, and round and round this yard the aborigine followed the horse, carrying the bridle destined to be slipped up and over the animal's ears, today, tomorrow, or sometime. One of them would tire first, and it would not be the aborigine. One would be worn of patience, and it would not be the man. Wearing only old dungaree trousers, Captain followed the horse with the tenacity of a dingo.

As he would not want to be interrupted, Bony saddled

the roan mare put at his disposal and rode from the yard
past the homestead and thus to the desert with Lucifer's
Couch ahead. He had asked for a quiet horse, and the
roan was certainly docile, in fact, too docile. She declined
to canter. She made it obvious that leaving the homestead
wasn't done at two o'clock in the afternoon. Having no
switch, Bony had to drum her ribs with his heels.

The sky was flawless. The air was motionless. The sun,
well past the zenith, gave black shadow to every ground
thing: shrub, grass tussock, sharp unevenness of sand
made by animal tracks. The green of the creek gums was
over-painted with opalescent tints. The line of creek gums
retired slowly to the left, but the gold nugget lying on the
horizon appeared never to draw nearer. Here again Bony
found himself in the Deceitful Land where distance is
either magnified or reduced, level land becomes low sand
ridges, and great sand dunes sink to become as level as a
billiards table.

He followed the well-defined track of motor wheels first
made by Scolloti's utility and subsequently by the motors
conveying the investigators. Maintained at a sharp walk
against her will, the roan brought Bony to the outer of the
three rings circling the Crater. This rock upthrust was
barely a foot above the general level, and sand filled the
declivities, and here the motor vehicles passed over without obstruction. It ran away to the south and to the north
as far as could be seen and appeared rule straight. It was
much like the Yellow Brick Road to Oz, badly in need of
repair.

The next or middle ring was as the same road, well
formed and needing only to be rolled and sealed. Rocks
had been removed to permit the passage of vehicles as the
average height above ground level was three feet. It was
here that Lucifer's Couch jumped from being a golden
nugget on the horizon to become a flat-topped, wide hill

of commanding front. Coming to it from athwart, the rays of the radiant sun upon it appeared as though a mass of golden nuggets had been thrown with force against a mound of pitch, the shadows actually being responsible.

On arriving at the inner ring, Lucifer's Couch seemed touchable although still a quarter-mile away. More man-labour had been done to make passable the crossing of this ring many yards in width and four to six feet high. That is at the outside edge, because along the inner side the wash of sand and earth debris lay almost level with the summit. The roan walked on and up the gentle ground slope to the foot of the massive front of golden rocks.

Bony there reined her to the south and thus proceeded to skirt the Crater wall, estimated to be one mile in circumference and until recently thought to be almost straight.

When with Howard on the wall or rampart, without much credit, he had noted that although the summit was almost level there was at one point a cleft or sinkage reducing the height at this point by fifty-odd feet. He rode on round the wall until opposite this cleft and here dismounted and neck-roped the horse to a stout desert jamwood.

He climbed the wall from rock to rock as walking up a steep stairway, and, on reaching the top of the lower section or cleft, he gazed again upon Lucifer's Couch and marvelled at the perfection of cosmic bombardment. The only living creature to be seen was the eagle which came over the wall, sailed down into the pit, and with merely a few slow wing-flaps rose to sail over the wall on the far side.

The bird was obviously on its beat, hopeful of finding an iguana or lizard drowsing in the warm sunshine, and idly Bony wondered if the great bird remembered those days the dead man lay there unprotected. The scrub trees about the central soak-hole appeared like ragged buffalo grass, and the lesser bush-trees on the circular slope down to it as spindly grass stems. Lucifer's Couch! It would have been unforgettable; the sight of Lucifer's Fall. A well-chosen place too. The isolation he felt on the summit of the wall, plus the feeling of remoteness from this majestic, and yet desolate, monument to a meteor, momentarily gave the feeling of complete nakedness.

He shrugged it away and brought his mind to work on the problem set him, and he tried to project his mind back in time and into the skull of the man who had selected this vast pit to receive the dead. Why carry the body up and over this wall and leave it down by the dry soak? To every compass point, save to the north, the desert lay bare beneath the sun to the unbroken rim of the inland plain, an horizon so sharp as to appear little more than a mile or two distant. There lay thousands upon thousands of square miles of arid wastes. Why had Cain not buried Abel where the crime had been done? Why bring the body to this Crater? And having brought it, why place it in the clear outside the soak for a wandering aircraft to fly over? Why not accept the concealment provided by the meagre scrub about the soak? It didn't square with the psychology of the white man, of the semi-civilised aborigine, or of the wild black man who inhabited the southern wastes.

One week prior to this day a man had said: "Our interests in this dead man are of varying importance. Mainly we want to know how he got into the locality without being observed and reported. We'd like to know what he was doing out there. We would like to know why he was murdered. Who murdered him doesn't concern us, for that is the police job: yours, not ours."

"Do you know who he was?"

"Yes," answered the man. "We have identified the body by the fingerprints, the dentures, the evidence of smallpox. Therefore, we are not interested in the question of identity. Do you grasp what we want of you?"

"Naturally, having been to school," Bony had replied, and walked out of the office lorded by the condescending type.

Now he argued that were he confronted with the problem of carrying a dead man over this gigantic wall he would select the place where the wall was lowest in the length of its circumference. That would be where he was sitting. He conceded that a white man or men either in haste or panic would not think of this, or would decide it better to struggle up the wall at the point reached rather than carry it a further half mile to mount at its lowest point. He was, however, confident that the wild aborigines would select this lowest point, or pass, because they would have no lubras with them to undertake the labour. White men or black men was the question he needed first to answer.

He stepped down from rock to rock to the floor of the Crater. It was clean of tracks until he proceeded some twenty yards toward the centre. Keeping at that distance from the wall, he completed the full circle. He visited the pegs, driven in the ground to mark the position of the body, and finally came again at the base of the wall at its lowest point. He had crossed countless tracks made by boots and naked feet, and he had made one discovery.

The native trackers, including Howard's, had known that the dead man was a white man. They had been instructed to look for the tracks of a white man or men, and, believing that no white man could be expert enough to leave no tracks, they hadn't bothered to examine the base of the crater wall. None had thought to look for proof where the wall had been crossed.

The man who could think like an aborigine and reason like a white man proceeded to test the theory that the dead man had been brought over the wall at its lowest point.

He mounted the wall, this time using his hands as well as his feet to bring his eyes closer to the individual rocks and the deeply shadowed crevices. Instead of climbing directly, he mounted in wide zig-zags to cover the entire area below the pass. His hands found what his eyes failed to see. The finger-tips felt the still sharp angles of splintered rock which rain and wind and sun had not completely eroded away, proving that the meteor must have fallen in recent times and not hundreds of years ago. The edges were not sharp enough to cut his fingers, and thus would not cut the feet of a wild aborigine.

He spent two hours climbing the wall, and, when again he sat and smoked in the cradle of the pass, his hands were sore and his legs ached. The sun was setting over the northern mountain summits, the arms of the ranges thrusting into the desert dressed in purple and dark blue. The westward face of the Crater wall was painted indigo, and that facing the setting sun purest gold.

Bony stood and faced the setting sun, now dancing upon a distant tor. His right hand rose to touch the left pocket of his tunic where reposed an envelope containing several fibres of what he was sure were of hessian, the material used for bags, the material used by the men who had brought the body to the Crater to wrap about their feet and thus reduce the depth of their imprints and the more efficiently to erase them.

The wild men would not use hessian bagging. They would not own hessian bagging were they so minded to use it.

The sun scorched the distant tor, and the neighbouring summits became a chain of pastel-tinted jewels. The light took the standing Bonaparte and transmuted him to gold; the gold of the rocks about him, and even his teeth, bared in a grin of triumph, for a second or two, were of gold.

He rode homeward in the twilight of this magic world, the thrill of detection carrying him onward as an empty belly urged the horse to run at racing speed. He had been able to eliminate the wild aborigines, for the fibres proved that men wearing boots had conveyed the body to the Crater. They would be white men, or aborigines employed as stockmen. They could have come from Deep Creek or from Beaudesert, distance lengthening the odds in favor of Deep Creek.

This evening a conversational point, with the Brentners and their two off-siders, was of a coming tour of the Kimberleys by a Federal Ministerial party, and Bony, not particularly interested in how public money is spent, retired fairly early. From the heavy suitcase he took a pair of woollen shoes, made with the wool on the outside and intended to permit the wearer to leave no tracks. Having then ordered his sub-consciousness to wake him at four, he slept until that hour.

It was moonless and cold when, with the woollen shoes slung from his neck by the thongs, he left the house and followed the Creek bank, wearing his ordinary riding boots. Above, the meteors were busy, and it was seldom that a full minute passed without at least one flashing into momentary brilliance. He was at the ford, where Howard and he had crossed the Creek, when the first herald of the new day beflagged the eastern sky.

The ford, the homestead, and Lucifer's Couch formed a rough triangle, each side three miles in length. Thus it was three miles to the Crater, and now wearing the sheepskin shoes, he had gained shelter among a clump of desert jamwoods less than a mile from the great wall when the light was strong enough to observe its shape.

It appeared drab and featureless. His attention was concentrated on Lucifer's Couch and on the tiny horse teth-

ered to that same scrub tree he had used the previous day.
He saw the man appear round the southern curve of the
wall and watched him free the horse and ride it at a hard
gallop back to the homestead.

It was information needed and expected. Before daybreak the man had ridden to the Crater, and then, as soon
as light permitted, he had tracked Bony's horse to the
jamwood to which it had been tethered and then had
tracked Bony to the wall and seen where he had climbed
it and gone down the far side. Doubtless he, too, had descended to the floor and found what Bony had done there.
He now knew of Bony's movements the previous afternoon, but would be ignorant of the major discovery of the
hessian fibres.

Returning to the Creek, Bony changed his wool shoes
for his boots and proceeded to the homestead, the wool
shoes compressed against his side under the coat. Were
interest maintained in his movements, he would be tracked
to the tree above the ford where he had made the change
and no farther.

The horse-yards were empty, and the horse he had seen
ridden must have been taken from the open paddock and
returned there. When sauntering across the compound to
the house, he noted several lubras about the laundry. Captain was coming from his room. An aborigine riding bareback was driving the working horses to the yard, and Bony
thought it likely this was the man who visited the Crater.
One of the lubras wore a blue ribbon in her hair, and later
he watched this young woman walking up the Creek, obviously following his tracks.

5

MESSRS. GUP-GUP AND POPPA

Prior to the establishment of the Deep Creek Cattle Station, the aborigines whose tribal grounds enclosed this section of country had their main camp at a permanent water-hole seventy miles to the west. On the homestead being built at Deep Creek—and the dam constructed to maintain a permanent supply of water—water was piped to an elbow of the Creek to encourage the aborigines to settle there. For them the advantages were proximity to a homestead and tucker, as well as stock work offering the young men. Further, according to Mrs. Leroy who was closer to them than the Brentners, the move was approved by Gup-Gup because the original camp site was too close to a white settlement with its destructive influence on his people.

They were a western offshoot of the Bingongina Nation and were loosely affiliated with the Musgrave Tribe, who belong to this same nation. At this period of the Crater mystery, their ancient Chief was called Gup-Gup, so spelt as coming closest to the aboriginal pronunciation.

Chief Gup-Gup ruled his people for many years prior to transferring to Deep Creek, the transfer being two decades after the falling of the meteor. As did the people of Hall's Creek, he saw it fall.

No one knew how old he was when Bony decided to visit him. His ragged white hair seemed to peep at one above the snakeskin band encircling his head. His shrunken chest was scarred with old cicatrices, as was his back with the totem of the frogmen. His arms and legs were merely skin-covered bones. He had borrowed much time, but his black eyes were the eyes of a young man.

This morning, as was customary, he sat before a small fire, tending it by adding sticks gathered and piled beside him by the lubras. At his back was his wurley, built of bark laid against a stick framework, for he scorned the white man's cast off corrugated iron and bags. He scorned, too, the white man's clothing, being naked save for the pubic tassel and the dilly bag suspended from the neck by human hair string. He sat because he was unable to crouch upon his heels. As he owned no teeth, his nose almost contacted his chin.

It was a warm day following the cool night, and the camp, comprising humpies of old iron and bags about the central point of the communal fire, was alive with the cries of happy children, the shouts of the women busy doing little of anything important. Men gossiped over smaller fires, proving that a camp isn't a camp without a fire. It was when the camp noises abruptly ceased that old Gup-Gup raised his head and saw, distant some fifty yards, the squatting figure of Inspector Bonaparte.

There came to the Chief the Medicine Man called Poppa. He was under fifty, of powerful build, rugged of features, and by no means without character when minus the septal-bone of his profession and the girdle about his head to raise the mop of greying hair. Wearing only a pair of drill slacks with a ragged hole at the right knee, Poppa was not a striking figure of mystery and authority this morning.

"He is not, and there he is, the policeman at the homestead," he said, loudly, anger flaming his eyes and making breathing fast. "He is the first to draw close without us knowing. It must be his lubra mother alive inside him."

"It could be so," Gup-Gup placidly agreed, and rearranged the glowing ends of five sticks to brighten his fire as though to give welcome to the visitor. "A white policeman would ride his horse among us, and ask his questions and shout his orders. This one comes with knowledge. This one asks permission to enter the camp of strangers. Have him brought in." Poppa shouted, and two young men went forth to greet the visitor. Gup-Gup said: "He is the one who brought the white-feller law to the killers of Constable Stenhouse. Cunning feller, this one."

Bony advanced with the two men trailing behind. At the front of the wide-brimmed slouch hat was the badge of the Western Australian Police Force. He was wearing a drill tunic. On the epaulets were three wide black bars, but what these represented only Bony himself knew. Gup-Gup and Poppa accepted them as the insignia of high rank. Come to them, Bony stared at the camp and the stilled inhabitants who faded into the background like gulls into the fog. He chose to squat on his heels, facing the two aborigines from the far side of the fire.

"My father and my mother and my uncle and my son, a long time back, spoke to me of you, Gup-Gup. Illawalli was the Chief of my mother's tribe."

"I have heard of Illawalli, of the Cassowary Tribe," admitted Gup-Gup without expression. "He lived and died far away." Approbation crept into his voice. "He left with you the customs of our people. Of you I have heard much. You witnessed the killing of Jacky Musgrave's killer: black-feller law. You found the killer of Constable Stenhouse: white-feller law. I know you were sealed by Illawalli." The ancient man again rearranged his fire-sticks, gazing moodily at them. Neither Bony nor Poppa spoke, and presently the Chief looked up to encounter the blue

eyes having such power that although they were not de-
feated they did not conquer.

"You know much," conceded Bony. He completed the
making of a cigarette and avoided the mistake of taking
up one of Gup-Gup's fire-sticks for a light. "I know much
too. I know why you brought your people to camp here.
That was good. I know you see many things of the future
in your fire. You know I am a big-feller white policeman,
not a black tracker. You know I can see to the back of
your head, and that in me is no fear of Medicine Men."

"I know that once long ago you were near boned to
death by the Medicine Man of the Kalshut Tribe," Gup-
Gup said.

This shook Bony as the Kalshut Tribe were sixteen hundred miles from the Kimberleys and the boning was done
fifteen years before. No sign of the thrust betrayed its effect. He was about to counter it when the less subtle and
experienced Poppa had to assert himself.

"In the Alchuringa Time there was a young man who
tongued his Medicine Man," interposed this modern speci-
men. "The Medicine Man took the young man's tongue in
his fingers and told him to run away and grow feathers on
it. The feathers became wings which lifted him up to the
branch of a tall tree. Then the tongue said: 'I'm tired of
all this flying about.' And the feathers all said: 'So are we.'
They all dropped out from the tongue, and the young man
fell to the ground and was killed."

"In the Time of Last Summer," Bony related in turn,
"there was a Medicine Man who poked out his tongue at
a white policeman. The white policeman took the hands
of the Medicine Man and put on them the manacles of
steel. Then he put the Medicine Man inside a baobab tree,
shut the door, and told him to break out if he could. Now
the Medicine Man, who had manacles on his wrists and
his ankles as well, was in a sore fix. He began to cry out

the boning curses upon the white policeman, and, while he was doing this, the manacles got hot and hotter and then turned to snakes that bit him into small pieces. And the small pieces escaped through a crack in the tree and went away dancing over the sandhills, and never more came together to make a Medicine Man."

From Gup-Gup issued a low chuckle.

"Poppa, you keep your tongue behind your teeth. The old men need your medicine. The young men need your fear. The lubras need your discipline. You couldn't tend to them from inside a gaol. I know. Long time ago I was in one." Again he chuckled. "The white policeman and his three trackers were very tired time they put me into the gaol. But they put me there." His voice became a whip. "Stop this lubra's cackling, Poppa. Big-feller policeman tell why he came here, eh?"

"As though you didn't know, Gup-Gup," Bony reproved. "I came for you to tell me about the man found dead in the Crater."

"That we don't know. He was a white-feller. Could be white-feller killing," calmly responded Gup-Gup, and as calmly withdrew one of his fire-sticks and with the red end prodded a six-inch centipede that had crawled from his wood heap.

"You don't know!" Bony echoed. "You can tell me who boned me fifteen years ago and on the other side of the world, and you can't tell me who killed the white-feller in the Crater. Seems this Tribe should get another Chief and another Medicine Man. Could be you two should be flung into gaol for a spell. You wouldn't escape in small pieces, and it wouldn't matter if you did because never would the pieces come together again to make Gup-Gup and Poppa."

The Medicine Man became absorbed in Gup-Gup's idle arrangement of his fire-sticks, and the Chief's hands betrayed the fact that fire-sticks were not at the moment of interest to him. He looked like an animated unwrapt mummy. He looked like a dirty bag of bones put together with wire and covered with dark-grey tights.

"You very cunning fellers, I know," Bony continued. "I'm a cunning feller too. White-feller law says no killing. You know that. I know, and you know I know, that that white-feller couldn't have been put into the Crater without you knowing about it. So don't talk like lubras and say you didn't know he was put there days before the plane people saw him. It's why you all went on walkabout that day the plane flew over."

"We went walkabout to initiation of our young men and lubras," stated Poppa.

"I was told that the tribe didn't have young men and women ready for initiation," argued Bony, knowing quite well that long preparation precedes actual initiation. "All right, you prove it, eh? You call the young men and the lubras here to prove it. Go on, bring them here for me to see. Their cuts wouldn't be old yet. Come on, Gup-Gup, stir yourself and order them to come here."

"It was not the time," answered Gup-Gup. "Our young men and women were not ripe. The initiation of the young men of Beaudesert was what we went walkabout for. Beaudesert fellers same as Deep Creek. They go walkabout, we go walkabout. White-feller law not against it. Constable Howard never told us stop always in camp."

"So it wasn't true about you going walkabout to initiate your boys and lubras. I say bring them here: you wriggle out like that centipede you killed." About Bony's face played a softly deceitful smile, and the two men saw it and ceased chewing their tobacco. "Of course it wasn't the right time. No faraway abo looking into his fire could have told you the plane would fly over the Crater. You didn't have time then to have your young people prepared. You knew when Constable Howard and I left Beaudesert to come to Deep Creek, for a black-feller looking into a fire told you, but there was no black-feller looking into a fire on that plane. So you didn't know it would fly over the Crater. Easy, isn't it?"

They were looking at his mouth rather than his eyes, and in their eyes was no expression. It was as though shutters had fallen before the glowing pupils, far more impenetrable than the so-called Iron Curtain. The effect was not to shut Bonaparte out, but to close themselves in, bar themselves against the intrusion of a foreign force threatening the citadel of a hoary culture. Bony had come against it so often he had long since recognised the futility of beating upon those mental shutters. He made another cigarette and smoked to the butt before saying: "You fellers could be pretty damn fools, not cunning fellers like you think. You are Chief Gup-Gup and you are Medicine Man Poppa, and between you you rule your people. You and your people live here with plenty of tucker. You live in peace for there is the white-feller law to say no one fight you and you must not fight anyone. You Gup-Gup can remember when there was always war and when your people fed well for short times and starved hard for longer times. You sit there in the warm and you remember how you have kept your people together blackfeller fashion, and how you have kept the black-feller law so that your people are ever happy.

"Why for all this? I'll tell you. Deep Creek say for you all to shift camp to this place. Plenty of water. Plenty of tucker. Your young men stockride for the Station and you all get plenty of tobacco. Hall's Creek a long way away. Fitzroy Crossing a long way away. Here at Deep Creek you can rule your people and Poppa can keep them obedient to the black-feller laws and customs.

"Not so the black-fellers at Broome, the black-fellers at Darwin. In those places the black-feller has become black-white-fellers. They're finished. You know that. You saw how that could be with your people if you hadn't come to Deep Creek. You know that in those places the black-feller puts out his tongue at his Chief, and he doesn't care a plug of tobacco for his Medicine Man. He goes from camp to camp, sleeping with this lubra and that one; he earns white-feller money he spends for dirty firewater. You know all that, the two of you."

Bony sighed and employed his fingers rolling another cigarette. They watched his fingers and met his eyes with their own shuttered against him.

"That dead white-feller gets himself killed," he went on, quietly. "He gets himself planted in the Crater. Someone put him in there because he didn't have wings to him. Now that hole in the ground belongs to you. It's on your country, not Beaudesert country. You tell me you are the Chief and you the Medicine Man, and then you tell me you don't know who killed that feller and who put him in the Crater. Why, you know how many eagles are flying over your country and who comes into it and who goes from it. And you know who killed that white-feller and who planted him.

"As I said, Gup-Gup, you could be pretty damn fools. White-feller law says that you are too big damn fools to run around here. Not me, but white-feller law put you both in gaol, and put your people some other place, and when you come out of gaol you will see your young men and the lubras poking their tongues out at you and telling your Medicine Man to go jump over a fence. That is if . . . I say if, Gup-Gup, and you, Poppa, were flung into gaol."

The ensuing silence was prolonged until the Medicine Man vented held breath and said: "White-feller nothing to do with us aborigines. Us aborigines nothing to do with him."

Silence took them again, strengthening still more the barriers separating this ancient people and the modern representative of an alien race. Bony smoked two more cigarettes before rising and walking back to the homestead.

6

THE LITTLE PETS

Bony was unperturbed by the apparent negative result of his call on Gup-Gup and his Medicine Man. Individually they ran true to type, and together had behaved normally.

Coincidentally, the power vested in a commanding officer and his adjutant over a battalion is roughly applicable to the government of an Australian Tribe, and as the battalion is the unit of an army division, so is the Tribe the unit of a nation. A soldier will agree that a well-run battalion is that governed by a martinet of a commanding officer, sugared by an adjutant who is popular with the men, or vice versa: a splendid balance being thus achieved.

Gup-Gup was the sugar and Poppa the vinegar in the diet of this Deep Creek tribe of the Bingongina Nation. In another tribe of this same nation the balance in command might well be reversed, while more often than not tribal rebellion is due to too much sugar or too much vinegar.

It was probable that Gup-Gup had been elected chief by the Old Men of his tribe on the demise of the previous office holder, and it was not unreasonable for Bony to put his term at seventy years, a period covering the change from the complete wild state to that of peaceful co-existence with the white race. The Chief would not be ignorant of the process of disintegration already beginning to threaten his people by the steady encroachment of civilisation, and, in fact, Mrs. Leroy who had enjoyed his confidence had been so informed.

As for Poppa, it was most likely he had been appointed to his office by his predecessor, having been especially trained for his singular attributes revealed in early manhood, and also having survived the severe physical trials set out by centuries-old custom. The white doctor cures with drugs and sympathy. Poppa would cure with herbs and fear. The white priest prevents much sin with the threat of hell fire: Poppa would curtail much back-sliding with the fear of the Kurdatia Man and the Great Snake. What Freud revealed by his writings, Poppa would have learned very early in his training.

Neither of these unwashed aristocrats was a fool: both would have been stoutly admired by Machiavelli. They would not incur the hostility of the law to evade responsibility for a minor crime committed by one of their people, such as stealing from a homestead store or killing a white man for interfering with a lubra. Bony was considering with growing confidence that the cause of the shuttered eyes was an abstract one such as loyalty to a white man, or men, or fear of a neighbouring tribe more powerful than they and less influenced by white-feller law.

These matters he reviewed while sitting on a log on the bank of Deep Creek overlooking the water dammed back by the concrete wall. The site was well chosen, for the Creek here had itself dug deeply at an elbow, permitting the water to extend for a hundred yards to the far side, and bank up round the bend above. Water beetles and other insects constantly ringed the surface of this dam, and, upon it, the shadows of the dancing leaves played silent music.

Bony had his back to the house and was unaware of Mister Lamb until determinedly nudged in the back, and a few moments after he had obliged Mister Lamb with a cigarette, he was joined by Rosie and Hilda Brentner. They sat either side of him and drummed their heels against the log.

"Are you looking at our dam?" asked Hilda.

"I was thinking how pretty it is with the water beetles hard at work and leaf shadows dancing on the surface. It looks deep, though. I suppose no one ever bathes here."

"Oh yes," replied Rosie. "We do. Not right down there. Up the Creek where the water is shallow. Old Ted's teaching us to swim. Tessa can swim, but she won't any more."

"Why ever not," Bony pressed.

"Well, she was swimming right down there one day when Captain came and saw her. And he laughed and teased her, and she wouldn't go in again, ever. Can you swim?"

"When I fall in. Your father and mother don't mind people swimming in the dam?"

"Oh no. There's plenty of rain water for the house in the tanks," replied Rosie, and Hilda further explained: "It comes down off the roof when it rains."

"I see. D'you play much with the little boys and girls from the camp?"

"Sometimes we do, Bony," Hilda said. "That's when we all go for a walk with Captain. He takes us out on the desert, and we all pretend we're tracking a Musgrave black. Alfie or someone is the Musgrave, and we track him, and he tries to throw us off by wiping out his tracks, and Captain shows us how to find them again."

"You like Captain, I can see."

"Captain's the most wonderful man in all the world, excepting Daddy," declared Hilda, and her sister took her up on this point.

"He's not. Old Ted is."

"He is not," vowed Hilda. "Captain beat him in the fight. We saw it."

Rosie slipped off the log to confront her sister and scold: "That's a secret. We promised Tessa never to tell. You know we did."

Little Hilda bit her lip and looked like crying, and Bony said that perhaps Tessa meant not to say anything of it to anyone at the homestead. As he wasn't anyone at the homestead, it wouldn't matter about the secret. This dried the tears before they fell, and he asked if they had any pets to show him.

Each took a hand and showed him Mrs. Bluey and her small puppies. From these they escorted him to a large aviary containing some hundred love birds, and then to call on Bob Menzies in his own yard, Mister Lamb following faithfully and now and then trying to jog his memory by nudging a leg.

"We saw you give Mister Lamb a cigarette," he was accused by Hilda.

"Did you now. He seems to like a cigarette."

"He likes cake tobacco too," supplemented Rosie. "He steals it off Jim if he can get into the kitchen without being seen. Steals the potatoes too."

"And what does Jim say to that?" enquired the enchanted Bony.

"He rushes Mister Lamb outside and tells him he's going to shoot him. Course he won't, you know. Would you like to ask Jim if he's baked raspberry tarts this morning?"

"Ooo! D'you think he would give us some? Let's try."

Approaching the kitchen they could see the door was open and Jim Scolloti working within. The little girls hung back with seeming bashfulness, and Bony advanced to plead with the cook. He was about six feet from the door when he was struck from behind with tremendous force. The ramming lifted him off his feet, and, without contacting the door frame, he was thrown into the kitchen where he landed on all fours at the cook's feet.

"That ain't no way to come into a man's kitchen," complained Jim Scolloti, walking round Detective Inspector Bonaparte as though interested in a pet crocodile. "Suppose it was that flamin' sheep what sort of shoved you. He's liable."

Dignity slightly ruffled, Bony stood and turned to look out the doorway. There was Mister Lamb eyeing him with satanic triumph, and beyond him were the two small girls gazing solemnly as though anxious to know the cook's verdict anent the raspberry tarts. Beginning to feel sore, Bony's sense of humour yet rescued him.

"The flaming sheep is decidedly liable," he agreed. "I've never been tossed by a bull, but the sensation must be something like. What I actually came for was to suggest that if you had baked raspberry tarts this morning you might be generous."

Scolloti's lively dark eyes appeared to flicker, and thoughtfully he pulled at his grey beard. On a bench behind him were several large dishes of various confectionery, and, to test a theory, Bony asked if this was his pastry-baking morning.

"Yes, Inspector, so it is," replied Scolloti. "Those imps know it too. What you came for was to be pocketted. I got pocketted once. Mister Lamb's the greatest snooker player in Orstralia."

"I'm beginning to feel I was pocketted by the greatest snooker player in Australia," Bony averred, and sat on a case beside the main table. The cook occupied a chair. His eyes flickered from the doorway back to Bony.

"You could call it billiards," he tendered. "I used to play soccer one time, so it could be soccer, but a soccer goal is a damn sight bigger than them door posts, and they're bigger than a table pocket. I've seen some good carom shots at billiards, but then Mister Lamb never makes no carom shot. Just as well, too, 'cos if he played carom shots a bloke's liable to be hurt bouncin' off a door post."

"Who instructed Mister Lamb?" Bony asked, still interested.

"An abo we calls Captain. The Boss brought the lamb off a sheep station when Rosie was beginning to crawl about. Time Rosie's trotting, the lamb's growed to a hefty wether, and she'd hang on to his wool and ride him everywhere he thinks to go. He'd eat anything from sweets to spuds, with tobacco and cake if he could pinch 'em. He got that way he could hardly stand, and we had to put him on a diet."

"You don't say," murmured Bony.

"I do say. We had to cut out sugar and pastry and such like, and increase his tobacco. But he gotta brain. One night he et the vegetable garden nigh clean out, and we found he could lift up the gate latch and push. Then one morning I comes in here and finds him laying in front of the stove. In the pantry I'd left about forty pounds of top-grade spuds, and there's not a spud left. They was all down his neck."

"Did he take to billiards by watching the players?" sceptically asked Bony.

Scolloti spread his hands and shrugged.

"You don't believe, but you will if you're here long enough. It was Captain who taught him snooker. He used to tease Mister Lamb and get him to chase after him. Once Mister Lamb caught him and sent him for a boundary. Then Captain got an idea. Them ruddy abos is full of ideas. Captain stuck two sticks in the ground, and made a straw man to stand between 'em. Then he gets astride Mister Lamb and aims him. In no time at all Mister Lamb gets that good the straw man can be pulled back a bit, and he can pocket it between the sticks. J'you know what?"

"What?" asked the enthralled Bony.

"I seen it meself. I was standin' about here opposite the door. I seen Captain making this way, and I seen young Rosie and the lamb away out. And she's aiming Mister Lamb at Captain. Well, you shoulda been here. He sends Captain right in without touching either side, and Captain lands against this far wall with his face. Served him right, and I told him so. And ever since that day Mister Lamb don't want to be aimed. He can do his own aiming at the drop of a hat. Never misses.

"Got me hard and proper as I told you. Got the Boss once. Got Old Ted, and a few more at odd times. You see, we're so used to him being around, we forget he's waiting for a chance to cue."

"He won't get a second chance at me," Bony said forthrightly.

"I don't know about that, Inspector. When Old Ted got pocketted he said that familiarity breeds contempt. That's about the sum of it."

"A truism, indeed. Do you think either Rosie or Hilda aimed Mister Lamb at me?"

"Don't think." Jim Scolloti pondered the problem. The bridge of his nose wrinkled, and his black eyes flashed to the open door. "'Course, I wouldn't put it past either of 'em to sort of nudge Mister Lamb's head to take a look at where you was going. Why don't you arrest 'em on suspicion?"

There was a flurry, and Rosie dashed into the kitchen to glare with blazing eyes up at the tall Scolloti. Hilda came to stand tremblingly behind her. Rosie's voice was shrill.

"I didn't aim Mister Lamb, Jim Scolloti. I wasn't anywhere near him. And you said just a minute ago he didn't want any aiming. You did so."

"Now don't you go getting your hair off, chicken," implored the cook. "I didn't say you did aim him, and you was both just outside the door listening, and heard what I said."

"Correct," Bony agreed officiously. "You say you didn't aim Mister Lamb at me, and I always accept the word of a lady. Now there isn't anything to it, is there?"

The anger faded from the brown eyes, and Rosie nodded and tried to smile. Scolloti exclaimed at the time and declared he'd get the sack if he didn't prepare the lunch, and would they all get out of his flaming kitchen.

Bony seized opportunity by the beard. He asked for raspberry tarts, and Scolloti gave two to each of them, and they strolled to the garden seat under a date palm, and silently munched. Then, having wiped his sticky fingers on a handkerchief, Bony spoke to Mister Lamb who was licking up the flaky crumbs and oddments of raspberry jam.

Little Hilda said, on the verge of tears: "Bony, I aimed Mister Lamb. I won't do it again."

7

WHAT DO YOU THINK
OF TESSA?

At dinner, Kurt Brentner gave a news flash.

"A bunch of politicians headed by the Minister of the Interior are on their way," he said. "Left Derby this morning by car. Intend to inspect the Kimberleys and the Northern Territory. They'll camp two nights at Hall's, and during their stay there'll be a conference with the pastoralists on the best ways of developing the North."

"Oh, shall you be going?" Rose asked, and her husband nodded. "We shall be going, if it suits you."

"It will be nice for them. Perfect camping weather," murmured Old Ted.

"Wonderful," agreed Young Col. "But what hardships."

"Oh, I don't know." Old Ted gazed sorrowfully at Brentner. "How many in the party?"

"Sixteen: totalling politicians plus secretaries, plus experts."

"Sixteen! Plus wives makes it thirty-two. That'll mean sixteen cars, sixteen drivers; two police guides in one jeep; cook and off-sider in a cook truck; two common men and truck with camp gear, said common men to erect and dismantle tents, etc. Something wrong somewhere."

Rose asked sweetly: "What, Mr. Iconoclast?"

"Only sixteen, Mrs. Brentner. Last year there were twenty-one. Year before nineteen. Year before that . . ."

"Trade recession," Young Col offered. "A hundred thousand people out of work proves it. Mustn't make too much of a splash or the hoi polloi might tear down the Bastille. Moderation is called for. Holidays for politicians must be spread wider than is usual. Do you think they'll leave the beaten track this time, Boss, and come down here? We could show them our Crater: introduce them to Mister Lamb."

Young Rosie struggled to suppress laughter, exploded, was frowned at by her mother who said with faint protest: "If the Canberra politicians don't come up here and hear of our problems, how can we expect them to understand our needs and to develop these vast, almost uninhabited, areas? I can see nothing wrong with it. Rosie, what is the matter? Why are you giggling?"

"It's Young Col's fault, mother. He made me see Mister Lamb pocketting the Minister."

Although amused, Bony did not enter the conversation on this subject of luxurious tours for politicians during the winter months of supremely beautiful weather. He lost interest when argument arose over the probable cost to the taxpayers, the number of winters such tours were made, and the number of years left before the Asians walked into the country and developed it without holidays for their politicians. Some were questions old Gup-Gup could have answered off-hand.

He studied Tessa and talked with Hilda, sitting beside him. The child had not joined her sister in merriment, and Bony induced her not to dwell hardly on her pricking conscience. Tessa, he noted, gave much of her time to the children who accepted her strictures with neither fuss nor objection. Her demeanour, her table manners, her dress sense were all tributes to Rose Brentner's care and affection.

Later this evening he had the opportunity to talk with

her and, having persuaded her over the hurdle of native reserve, found her most responsive to his leads. She told him that at the beginning of the following year she was to go down to a Teachers College in Perth, and that she was looking forward to the adventure although sure she would greatly miss home life at Deep Creek. She wanted to know of his educational attainments and about his family, as Rose Brentner had told her something of it.

"When you graduate from college, I understand you will return to teach the local children. That right?"

"Yes, Inspector. We are hoping to do what Mrs. Leroy did, and go farther than she was able. Mr. Brentner says he will build a schoolhouse. It's always been my ambition."

"Splendid! I was talking to Gup-Gup this morning. D'you think he'll agree to it?"

A tiny frown puckered her fine brows for a moment, and her large and expressive eyes reflected determination. She said: "He'll have to. We'll make him, and Poppa. They think they can keep the Tribe from being assimilated for ever. How can they? This North country will have to be developed soon, and more and more people will come here to settle. Even the politicians are reading the writing in the sky."

Bony looked at the girl from a new angle. There was nothing vulgar, loud, or brash either in speech or appearance, nor was there even a hint of the female aborigine's reticence to talk openly to a man.

"You are a remarkable girl, Tessa," he told her, and the compliment she accepted with natural ease. "You know, there have been situations in my career when I've found myself acting as a kind of bridge spanning the gulf between the aboriginal and the white mind. If you realise your ambition you might well build a far stronger bridge, because you are thinking as a white woman. How often do you visit the camp?"

"Oh, I go along to see my mother sometimes. She isn't very well. If it wasn't for her I'd go there very rarely. I wonder if you know why?"

"Perhaps I do. May I guess?"

Tessa nodded, and he fancied he saw pleading in her eyes.

"I am only half black, and yet I, too, have felt the pull toward my mother's race. It's tremendously powerful as witness its effect on so many promising aborigine scholars. The strongest weapon I have to use in defence is pride. Pride in my career, in my sons, and in my wife, who is like me. I've never failed to finalise an assignment. I shall not fail with this one. Pride is the only rock I have to hold to. Is my guess right?"

Again she nodded, and it happened she sat sideways to the light and he was unable to be sure that shutters had dropped before her eyes. With no trace of alarm in her voice, she said: "Yes, you are right, Inspector. I thought you would know, and I believe your weapon is the only one. I've had to use it so often."

"The farther you go in your chosen career the easier it will be to wield, Tessa. I'll tell you what you could do to strengthen your arm. Come to regard your people objectively, and you could do that by writing a history of the Tribe before old Gup-Gup dies and takes it all with him. Ever thought of that?"

"Yes, I have," she replied. "I began to plan it, and then I found out that Captain is attempting it, and I left it to him and compiled a book of legends. I am still adding to it, and I was hoping you'd find time one day to recount many I don't know."

"Surprise on surprise," Bony told her, lightly. "I'd be glad to. And Captain is writing a history! I must persuade him to let me look at that. And your collection of legends, too, if you will. It would seem he is much closer to the

WHAT DO YOU THINK OF TESSA?

Tribe than you. Is he as advanced in education as you are?"

Tessa required time to formulate the answer, and Bony was happy knowing she was being careful.

"He reads a lot," she said. "He writes a wonderful hand. But he hasn't the weapon you have, and I found I have. Yes, I'd like you to see my legends, and thank you for consenting to add to them. Mine are mainly on the northern tribes, with one or two of the Ilpirra and none of the Orabunna."

Bony betrayed nothing of the slight irritation he felt when Old Ted crossed the room to join them with the remark that the interrogation by the Great Detective had continued long enough, but when he went off to bed he was delighted by the evening.

At breakfast, taken in the outside day-house, he chose to sit between Young Col and Old Ted. The men only were present, the women having their breakfast later as was customary. Also as is customary, after the first greeting, the men seldom spoke until they fell to loading a pipe or making a cigarette. It was Kurt Brentner who said: "Better ride out to Eddy's Well, Col, and look-see to the mill and tanks." He glanced at the red-bearded man. "You mentioned saddle repairs, Ted. You might do some of it while tending to the pumping engine. Tanks are getting low, and the garden ought to have another soaking. Tessa and the kids can do that. They like paddling around."

"Work!" moaned Young Col. "A man's work's never done. I work my fingers to the bone for you, Boss. There's no fun in life. Even the Minister won't call and meet Mister Lamb. Wish I were a detective, just lolling about and trying to jerk the grey matter."

"You might like me to ride with you today," Bony said. "I can be pleasant company."

"Better than my own, pal. It's a bet. Now you've dealt it out, Boss, what are you going to do?"

"Read a love romance on the verandah and take an occasional sip of canned beer," replied the Manager, and Young Col appealed to his fellow slave.

"What d'you know?"

"Between tending the pump engine and mending the saddles, I'll turn the pages for him and help him bend his elbow."

"You do that. We mustn't let him overtax his strength." Brentner grinned good-naturedly at Bony, and the young man added: "I'll collect the lunches, Bony. See you over at the yards."

"Are you seeing any light?" Brentner asked Bony when Old Ted and Col had left. "What are you thinking about this business at the Crater?"

"I visited the camp yesterday," Bony said evading the issue. "I talked to Gup-Gup and Poppa. How old d'you think Gup-Gup is?"

"A hundred. Must be. All the time I've known him he sits at his little fire. Does nothing else. The Medicine Man's a loafing scoundrel if ever there was one. Still, I leave both of 'em to Captain."

"Taking the camp as a central point, is this Eddy's Well the nearest watering place for your cattle?"

"On the desert side, yes."

"A well and mill farther out?"

"Yes. Place we call Dead Man's Drop. Thirty-odd miles beyond Eddy's. Then coming round to the south-east there's Bore Number Three, and then Paradise Rocks close to seventy miles south of the Crater. If you go out there you'll get a surprise. Permanent water surrounded by acacias. Not safe, though. The wild blacks claim it's theirs."

"I must visit these places," Bony decided. "Just between us, Gup-Gup and Company could tell something about the mystery man in the Crater. Well, I'll go with Young Col. See you later."

"Good! Ask Col to tell Captain to turn the yarded horses out into the paddock, will you? I didn't think of it."

Young Col was saddling up when Bony joined him and conveyed Brentner's message. Young Col shouted it to Captain who then left his work on the current youngster and came to the yard rails.

"You met Captain, Inspector?" Col asked.

"No. I watched him at work the other day. How do, Captain! They keeping you busy?"

The aborigine, who could model as a Greek Olympian, grinned and said some horses could think and the one in hand was a thinker and being stubborn. His round face was creaseless, his eyes bold and now almost merry. He asked where they were off to and Bony told him.

They rode into the desert, sometimes cantering, sometimes walking the horses close. Young Col explained that Deep Creek continued its course for seven miles before emptying its flood waters over a huge area to the southward, this area covered with buffalo grass, criss-crossed by water gutters, supported box and other trees, the whole desolate and depressing. At the southern extremity was Eddy's Well, and it was easier riding to proceed direct than follow the Creek.

Crossing the great elbow of the desert gave the sense of nakedness induced by limitless spaces. Here grew the spinifex, and stunted jamwoods, the porcupine grass in large clumps, all separated by wide areas of light-red sand. To the south rose a line of yellow sand dunes cutting beautifully into the rim of the brilliant sky. The homestead and its buildings sank from view behind them, and after three hours they could see ahead the windmill and reservoir tank at Eddy's Well at the southern tip of the grass country.

Cattle had eaten out the grass about the Well for half a mile. The troughs, two of them, ran outward from the linked reservoir tanks lorded by the windmill, which itself dwarfed the low iron shed housing the pumping engine, for use when the wind failed for long periods. On the north side of the Well, and two hundred yards from it, stood an open-fronted shed with its back to the west winds, and close by a small horse-yard. As Young Col said, a depressing place.

"Can be either good or bad," he enlarged when they were eating Jim Scolloti's lunch at the fireplace several yards in front of the shed. "I was stationed here once for two weeks, and it nearly drove me up the wall. It wouldn't happen, of course, when the Creek ran a banker for a week, and all through this grass country the small lakes and gutters were black with ducks. Got here one day and saw what no one could forget. Old Ted and I came out next week with guns. Filled a couple of sacks with ducks. When they got up the sun went out. She was terrific."

"You like the life, though, don't you?"

The hazel eyes gleamed with enthusiasm, and the fair hair was tossed back from the broad forehead.

"My dad owns a couple of sheep properties down in Vic.," Col said. "Wanted me to go in for sheep: manage a place eventually. I wanted to see Australia first. Got this far and been here ever since. To hell with sheep on the Riverina. Cattle and old Brentner will do me."

"What about city life?" asked Bony. "What about the girls and bright lights? Don't you hanker after them?"

"When I was stuck here for a fortnight, I surely did, Bony. This ruddy country gets a man, all right. Last time I went down to Melbourne for a spell, I ached to get back again. Suppose I'll have to go down for keeps some time or other. Please the Great White Patriarch. Old Ted's father and mother were killed in a car accident, so he's got nothing to go back to. Inherited a lot of dough, though. The Kimberleys have got him, like they've got me and Brentner, even Mrs. Brentner." Then he asked: "What do you think of Tessa?"

8

YOUNG COL'S PROBLEM

"I haven't given much attention to Tessa," Bony said, wondering at the sudden change of subject no less than the question. Young Col was sitting cross-legged on the ground, the expiring campfire between them. Now he didn't look years younger than his age, and the cheeky attitude to life was replaced by a thoughtful study of Bony.

"I mean where d'you think she's going?" persisted Col. "Mrs. Brentner is set on sending her to a Teachers College, and all that. I don't doubt she'll pass out qualified. Then what?"

"The general idea seems to be that when she has qualified she'll return and begin teaching. Here, I presume. What's on your mind?"

"Well, what do you think about a white man marrying a black woman?"

"I don't approve of mixed marriage," replied Bony, still puzzled. "The woman I married is like me. We suffer at times from condescension, sometimes from sheer rudeness."

Col's eyes were small and in them lurked anxiety.

"Go on," he urged.

"Well, you are twenty years old, I understand, and Tessa is, say, eighteen. A good age to marry . . . But, you being white and Tessa being black, the inevitable outcome would be that in ten years when you would be thirty and Tessa twenty-eight, you would be going on to the prime of life and Tessa would have arrived at the prime of life. Add a further ten years. . . . You see that, don't you?"

"Yes, I see it all right."

Col Mason rolled a cigarette, the while watching the thin spiral of smoke rising from the almost dead fire ash. Bony waited, thinking of another young man who found the problem unsolvable.

"It would, of course, be marriage or nothing," Bony continued. "Even should the Brentners give their consent to marriage, there would still be the State to settle with. Association out of wedlock would be disastrous for you."

Col glanced up to encounter the sympathetic blue eyes.

"For me! I wasn't talking for myself. It's Old Ted I'm thinking about. You see, Old Ted's a goner on Tessa. He's a decent bloke, and I'd hate to see him fall over his feet. Then it's sort of complicated as Captain has ideas about Tessa too. Tessa adds her bit to stir those two up, and sometimes I get worried over Old Ted."

"I understand they had a fight. Was that over Tessa?"

"So you know about that?"

"Yes. I know about that. It seems to be a secret, though."

"We kept it dark from the Brentners. Captain was too good for Ted. Made a mess of him, and we cooked up the tale that he was thrown from his horse and had his foot caught in the stirrup and was dragged some ways. That fight was brought on by Tessa. You wouldn't think . . ."

"Fights have been brought about by school teachers, Col."

"You wouldn't think Tessa was a scheming bitch, would you?"

"No." Bony forebore to chuckle. "You know, Col, girls of seventeen and eighteen, and women of forty or fifty are what you said. A woman is always scheming about some man or other. Tell me more about Little Miss Muffet."

"You'll keep it dark?"

Bony nodded.

"I don't think the Boss subscribed a hundred per cent to the foot-in-the-stirrup yarn," Col went on. "Don't ask me. I've the feeling that Captain wasn't hotted up enough to fight Ted, and that the Boss did the final stoking to put Ted in his place. He's a cunning cove, Brentner. Course, the Boss might have been sooled on by Mrs. Brentner to sool Captain on to Ted. Something like that."

Bony thought this theory plausible, and said so, but returned to Tessa.

"Tessa knows how to ravish a bloke, Bony. You know, looks at you with both eyes wide open and an adoring look in 'em. Tried it on me more than once. I've seen her working on Ted. She's one of those tabbies who has to work on a man or burst."

"And you think something is going to burst, anyway?"

Slowly Young Col nodded.

"One reason why I was disappointed this morning when Brentner said the politicians wouldn't be coming to Deep Creek was that if they came and stopped a night or two they'd take minds off a girl who's firing a couple of pots," he said, thoughtfully. "Then when the Boss told us he would be going to Hall's for the conference, that meant he'd take Mrs. Brentner and the kids with him, and that Ted would go, too, and perhaps me as well. That would leave Tessa with Captain, and Old Ted would know that, of course."

"When did the fight occur?"

"Couple of weeks after the last mustering."

"Were you present?"

"No. I found Ted cleaning his rifle, and saw his face and he told me. He was that mad I was sure he was going to do some shooting. Goes berserk. Completely loses his block when he gets that way. I had trouble calming him down and getting him to agree with the stirrup yarn to account for his condition. I have a lot of time for Ted, you understand. Only real cobber I've ever had."

Following a period of moody silence, Bony made the suggestion that it might be wise to put the problem to Brentner, and to this Col said he was sure Brentner's solution would be to sack Old Ted as he couldn't get rid of Captain.

"Brentner's solution could be to send Tessa off to the College," countered Bony.

"Don't think," argued Col. "She's not ready. Anyway, Mrs. Brentner wouldn't agree to it."

"A string covered with knots, Col. We shall have to give thought to undoing the knots. What's your opinion of Captain?"

"Give him an inch, takes a yard. Thinks he's next to the Boss. Hellish good with horses, though. Keeps the abos in order. We want stockmen, he sees to it we get them. I've never taken to him. No particular reason."

"To go back to the fight. What brought the pots to the boil? What triggered it?"

"Why, the skirt," replied Young Col; then realising he was using a "square" word, hastily added: "The black baby, of course."

"You mistake me," objected Bony. "The black baby was the cause, but what was it which triggered the effect?"

"Oh, I see what you mean." Col frowned at the dead fire ash. Bony idly regarded the horses, idly until his mind registered their interest in something beyond the line of his vision. "I don't know what triggered 'em, Bony. The pots had to come to the boil sometime, I suppose."

"Not necessarily, Col. The pots could simmer on and on and never boil over. Are there any horses out here?"

"No. I can't think what could have brought about the fight."

"Try. Think back before the fight. The fight came about two weeks after you returned from the muster, remember."

Young Col pondered, and Bony noted that the horses' interest in what had captivated them had passed. Farther out from the mill a long line of cattle was approaching. The trees standing on clean ground stood as though painted on canvas. In the distance where the grass grew under the ragged and ugly gums they appeared to be standing on melting snow. A crow whirled by and circled to perch on the mill and there give tongue to defiance. Col was still hunting in his storehouse of memories when the horses again became interested in the grass at the rear of the two men. Softly, Bony said: "There could be someone behind the shed. Ready to investigate?"

Then he was on his feet and racing for the corner, leaving Col still grappling with the answer concerning the fight. Bony ran round one end of the shed to see fleeing from it across the clear ground to the trees and the grass the naked figure of an aborigine. Turning about he collided with Col, and, following the shock, ran to the horses. Give the young man his due, he was tightening the saddle girth under his horse when Bony slipped the saddle from his filly and rose to straddle the bare back. He was a hundred yards away after the running aborigine when Col was riding. Only to see Bony give up the chase as the aborigine plunged almost headfirst into the grass at the height of a man's shoulders.

Bony criss-crossed the direct line to the shed, and thus picked up the aborigine's tracks proving the man had come from the grass to the shed where he laid himself down close to the rear wall.

"A wild black," exclaimed Col. "First time I ever saw one this far north. Could be others about. They might be

planning to spear a beast. They do sometimes, you know,
but not this far north. It'll slay the Boss. He reckons he
came to a sort of agreement with 'em."

"How?" pressed Bony, dusting his ill-used saddle and
placing it on the filly, still a little excited.

"There's a beaut rock-hole with permanent water about
seventy miles south of the Crater. We leave a beast there
in a brush yard twice a year for the wild blacks to slaugh-
ter, and they leave our herds alone. Saves them chasing
after a herd and spearing half a dozen to get one, like they
did here when they wounded nine and ate only a quarter
of one of 'em."

"And who contacted the wild men to make that treaty?"

"Captain and Gup-Gup." Col regarded Bony nervously
when adding: "You won't believe it, perhaps, but old Gup-
Gup looks into his fire and radios. Takes believing, but
there's something to it, I think. Lots of yarns up here that's
a bit tall."

"I can imagine," Bony replied, and mounted. Later,
their jogging horses close, he said: "That aborigine might
have been one of Gup-Gup's crowd."

"Aw, I don't know," objected Col. "Gup-Gup's crowd
don't run around naked. Boss wouldn't have it. He'd go
to market if he thought one of them was out to kill a beast.
There wouldn't be a logical reason for that. They get all
the beef they can eat."

"I was thinking it likely that that abo was trying to listen
to what we were saying. He walked from the grass to the
shed, keeping the shed between himself and us."

"Listening to what we . . ." Col broke off to ponder
with a heavy frown. He rode with deceptive looseness the
strong brown gelding he forked, and which, like the filly,
was smartly walking, knowing they were on the return to
the yards and freedom. He said: "'Fraid I can't buy that."

Deciding not to press the point, yet convinced that the

aborigine was not of a party to spear cattle at the Well,
Bony rode on and also pondered. It did appear that the
odds were many against the assumption that any one of
the local Tribe would be so interested in what they said as
to travel fifteen miles from the camp. And on foot if the
Tribe hadn't a horse. He asked about this, and Col said
they had no horses of their own.

"Does the Boss lend them a horse now and then?"

"Don't think," replied Col. "What'd they want to bor-
row a horse for? The bucks get enough riding with us."

Fifteen miles on foot out here and fifteen miles back to
the Creek surely did stretch the odds. The horses were
keen to be back, and Bony allowed his to break into an
easy canter, Col following behind and bursting into a song
about a Baby on Fifth Avenue he lurved with all his aching 'art. A swoony tale, it was possible that it laid balm to
Young Col's sad mood. Bony wouldn't know. His mind
followed a train of thought, and the sequence was severed
when Col stopped his dirge and shouted, bringing Bony
to rein his horse to a halt to permit the young man to catch
up with him. He was no longer sad.

"Hey, I've an idea you could be right," he said. "That
black bastard could have been listening to us. He could
have been sent out by Captain to fox us. And that reminds
me about how the fight was triggered off. I remember
now. I thought there was something I should have remembered."

As Col wanted encouragement to state his bright re-
covery of memory, Bony rolled a cigarette and waited.

"Yes, now I remember, Bony, what made the pots boil
over. Old Ted wouldn't say, but I'll bet it was because he
suspected Captain had put a lubra or someone to keep an
eye on him all the time to see if he went after Tessa. That'll
be it. Ted did say something about everything was told to
Captain. And then . . . Yes, I remember, too, when we

were in the Crater looking for tracks that Ted pointed out neither of us was ever free of a tail."

"When looking for tracks following the discovery of the body, I take it?"

"Yes." They rode on, and the silence that fell between them lasted for ten or eleven minutes.

"When we were saddling up this morning, there were eleven working hacks left in the yard," Bony said thoughtfully. "By now they would have been returned to the horse paddock. We'll see if one is missing. You would know them, I take it?"

"Oh yes! What's clicking?"

"Let's check if one has recently been galloped home ahead of us. And by the way, do me a personal favor, will you?"

"Why not?"

"No reason why not. Keep our interest in that eavesdropping abo to ourselves until I spring it."

9

CAPTAIN'S PRETTY LEGEND

The fenced horse paddock was one square mile in area, and at the far side was a gate to which Bony and Young Col rode, and thus rode through the paddock to the horse-yards adjacent to the homestead. In this paddock there were now ten horses when there should have been eleven, and Young Col named the missing animal a gelding called Star.

Captain was too intent on his work to note the audience of two who climbed up the rails of the yard to perch on the topmost one in time-honoured fashion. Half an hour later when he did see them, he grinned appreciatively.

"You can handle them, Captain," Bony praised justifiably, and the aborigine climbed to sit beside him and busy himself making a cigarette.

"The Boss says I mesmerises them before the handling," stated Captain. "I told him if Mesmer was alive he would do as good. What d'you think, Inspector?"

"An affinity with the animal. You all have that. Even I."

"You might like to give me a hand tomorrow with a proper swine of a filly. She's going to extend me. She'll probably keep me walking around for a week."

The softly spoken words were climaxed with soft laughter at himself, but beneath the laughter was the challenging hint of superiority with an unbroken horse.

"I would not like," countered Bony, also laughing softly

at himself. "I am getting old and tired in the legs. Chased a wild abo today, and he left me standing."

"A wild feller, eh! Where was he?"

"At Eddy's Well. Of course, he might not have been as wild as he looked because he carried no spears or waddy. Any of your people get around like that?"

"Out at Eddy's Well! Not at Eddy's Well or on the Creek, Inspector. A wild feller, surely. Did you see him, Col?"

"Going for his life," agreed Young Col, cautiously. "Dived into the grass like a good 'un."

"Not so good," said Captain. "Could be others with him. You tell the Boss?"

"Only just got back," answered the tutored Col. "Anyway, I'm not certain he was a wild black. His hair looked too short for one. What d'you think, Inspector?"

"I didn't notice," answered Bony guilelessly. "Anything unusual for a wild black to be as far north as Eddy's Well?"

"They get around sometimes," Captain said with seeming indifference. "I'd better tell the Boss, anyway."

Also with apparent indifference, Bony said: "Yes, you do that, Captain, while I trot along and talk with Gup-Gup and Poppa. By the way, how did the Medicine Man come to be tagged with that name?"

Captain heaved himself off the rail to the ground and opened a gate to free the horse into another and smaller paddock. Bony found Col looking at him and he signed to the young man to leave for his quarters. He proceeded to the aborigine's camp. He was but halfway when Captain caught up to him.

"Look, Inspector, why worry old Gup-Gup about this wild black? Gup-Gup's a hundred not out. He's too old to worry about anything."

"I am drawing nigh to a hundred not out," Bony

snapped. "I don't like worry, either. What do you suggest?"

"Well, it's like this," Captain said, halting. "I'm a sort of Public Relations Executive." Bony's brows shot upward. "I can read books, you know. I went to school for years. I don't roll in the dust at a campfire at night just for something to do. Now you tackle Gup-Gup about a wild black being out at Eddy's Well, and Gup-Gup's going to order a walkabout when the Boss'll be looking for half a dozen blacks to help in the re-thatching. Neither you nor Young Col are sure it was a wild black. It could have been a station black out there with a young lubra, and if Gup-Gup gets to hear about that there will be trouble. And my job's to stop trouble before it begins."

Bony pretended indecision.

"It could be as you say, Captain. Yes, it could have been one of the bucks out there with a young lubra. It has happened, hasn't it? They could have had a camp in the grass, and he could have been at the well for water. H'm! It's not my job to stir up trouble with station aborigines. I'd be slated for it. Think we should keep it from Mr. Brentner?"

"No, but you could leave it to me, Inspector. Station business: a problem like this. He'll probably say leave well alone." A slow smile spread over the not unattractive face. "Can't help bringing out old clichés. The Salvo Padre at Derby was down on them, but we learned them quick."

They had been standing, and now Bony produced tobacco and papers and squatted on his heels. Captain also squatted, apparently not unwilling and under the impression that Bony would no longer be difficult.

They rolled cigarettes, and each waited for the other to open the next phase, the one craftily conveying the impression of ineptitude; the other convinced he had to deal only with a white-police-trained half-caste, and therefore to be held in contempt by both white and black.

"I think we might do a deal, you and I," began Bony, looking up from lighting the cigarette. "Brentner was telling me you're a valuable liaison officer and that he owes much to you for managing the bucks on station work. To balance that, from your own words I get the conviction that the Tribe owes a lot to Brentner and his Company. That seems to be the position. Correct?"

"Yes." Captain held his burning match by the cold clinker end and watched the flame consume the other end. "You were telling Gup-Gup of the wasting away of tribal customs and discipline among the abos being assimilated. You weren't the first. I've been at him and Poppa too. I went to school in Broome, and I saw then what's going on, although only a kid. The Padre wanted me to take up mission work. D'you know what? I refused because the way of the white is bad compared with the way of the black man in this country."

"It's a long road," admitted Bony.

"It sags in the middle. The abo leaves his state and walks downhill, and he might, I say he might, walk up again to the white state. But the end of the road is always lower than the beginning for the aborigine. You must agree."

"I do, but there is no other road for the aborigine, and civilisation insists that he take it."

"Which is why civilisation must be defied as long as possible." Captain's dark eyes probed in effort to read what lurked in Bony's mind. "Tessa says you're interested in legends. I'll tell you one. In the Days of the Alchuringa there was a great scientist, and with the earth of a beautiful garden and his own spittle he made a man. Then he made a woman, and the woman always walked before the man.

"One day when the great scientist went into the garden to talk with the man, it was the woman who came first, the man being ashamed and hiding behind her. This angered the Creator, and He ordered that the front doors of the Garden be opened and the man and woman thrust outside. A day or so later, the Creator was walking sadly in his Garden when He beheld an aborigine approaching and behind this man was an aborigine woman. The Creator asked how they got into His Garden, and they said that when He banished out the front door those two white people, they crept in by the back door. He let them stay because always the woman walked behind the man, as it is to this day."

"You made up that legend," Bony said, and Captain nodded, saying while pointing toward the camp: "There still remains a tiny piece of the Garden. Mrs. Leroy used to say that the Garden exists in a man's heart, that he can tend it or banish himself from it. The white man says to hell with all that. I own the country, and these black people must be raised up and integrated with my civilisation. He actually believes that his way of life is better than ours: he can't understand that we don't want to be dragged from the Garden he once lived in, we don't want to be dragged down to his level."

"Did Mrs. Leroy tell you the story of King Canute?"

"Yes, she did," replied Captain. "A good legend too."

"King Canute's sea is the white civilisation in Australia today. It cannot be kept back. But enough, Captain. We're getting ourselves bushed. We agree on so many points that I wonder if we could agree on another. I think that Gup-Gup must know who carried the body of the white man into the Crater. Can we agree there?"

"Yes, I think he knows that, Inspector."

"Then for the good of his people, should he not say what he knows?"

"Of course not. I said just now that the whites want to drag us down to their level, and Gup-Gup isn't going to help them do it. I wouldn't inform if I knew. I never put it to Gup-Gup. I don't want to know. That affair had nothing to do with us. My job is to keep my people free. They are my people. One day I shall be their Chief."

"You strive to maintain the status quo?"

Captain nodded, and Bony was sure he knew the meaning of the phrase. He was a revelation. The aborigines have produced ministers of religion. They have produced teachers. This man had chosen another mission: to save his tribe as long as was possible from the degradation of being assimilated into the white civilisation. Bony said as much, and Captain frankly agreed.

"Then my mission here is a threat to your mission, is it not?"

"No, I don't think so, Inspector." Captain gazed away to the camp and repeated his opinion as though to reassure himself.

"My mother having been of your race, I shall be sorry if it becomes so," Bony said, and again encountering the black eyes, found them shuttered against him.

10

CAPTAIN STAGES A PLAY

While changing for the evening, Bony thought of the encounter with Captain and what Captain might have become had he been able to loosen even fractionally the tribal bonds. He recalled blind Mrs. Leroy, seeing her seated with her hands clasped on her lap and speaking of Captain as though he were her own son in whom she had had such hope and had been given only disappointment. Then there was Tessa who superficially had broken the tribal links which yet might prove too strong.

Having primed Young Col to say nothing of the missing horse and support the theory that the aborigine behind the shed was a wild man until something developed to prove otherwise, Bony had dressed leisurely and so found Kurt Brentner and his white stockmen in the day-house waiting for the dinner gong. It was obvious they were discussing the Eddy's Well incident, for Brentner at once asked for his opinion.

"The fellow was entirely naked, even the pubic tassel being absent," he said. "He carried no spears or other weapon which seems to blur the picture of a wild aborigine. Anyway, a moment before coming in I observed a party of aborigines approaching as though they were a deputation. As I talked with Captain shortly after we returned, perhaps he has found the answer."

"He might at that. He's no fool, Bony."

Captain appeared in the doorway. He had changed his old trousers for smart drill, and was wearing a clean white shirt. His hair was combed and on his feet were canvas shoes. Brentner called: "What's to do? Come on in."

"After Inspector Bonaparte spoke to me about the aborigine seen at Eddy's, I made enquiries at the camp," Captain began. He betrayed no nervousness, no hesitancy, no shuffling of feet. "With the help of Poppa, I found that young Lawrence and Mary's daughter, Wandin, had left camp four days ago. They've been camped in the grass half a mile from the Well, and Lawrence says he went there for water, got as far as the shed when Young Col and Inspector Bonaparte appeared and trapped him there. There's nothing much to it as they're to be married black-feller fashion next month. They beat the gun, that's all." Captain smiled, and the cattleman grinned. "Poppa says he'll deal with them. They're outside in case you'd like to talk."

Brentner nodded, and there appeared the Medicine Man with a young aborigine and a younger lubra. The lubra was wearing what looked like a nightdress much too large for her, and Poppa in old baggy trousers and no shirt failed to achieve the distinction of his rank. Indicating the sinners, he said: "This Wandin and this Lawrence feller been away from camp three nights, Boss. Wandin's mother started yowling. She's to blame. She shut her eyes, and the young men shut their eyes about Lawrence clearing out with Wandin. They came back at sundown. They broke a taboo, and the penalty will be put on them, never you bloody well fear."

Poppa was magnificent in outraged sense of the decencies. The girl began to snivel, and the lover tried to dig his toes into the hard floor. He was sullen, and Poppa roared: "You stop that yowling, Wandin."

Brentner rose from his chair and slowly advanced to

stand immediately before the couple. He spoke softly and with a bite in his voice.

"Lawrence, my lad, I'm leaving you to the tribal laws and penalty. What the penalty is I don't want to know. You're a good cattleman which is all I need to know. But you're a fool, Lawrence. White-feller law would have done nothing if you had been shot like a dingo. Wild black-fellers have no business at Eddy's, and you had no business getting around like one. You know that. You know we won't stand for you camp fellers running about naked. Only Gup-Gup can do that, and he don't wander off with young lubras no more." Swinging aside to face Poppa, he raised his voice to add: "I'm relying on you to see to it that your people don't run around with nothing on."

He returned to his chair, and Captain motioned to the entrance. The sinners slunk away, and Poppa stalked after them. Bony watched their figures fading into the fast falling night, saw them disappear towards the compound gate. He heard Captain say: "A sliver of wood under a knee-cap will stop them running off like that again. There'll be no more trouble, Boss."

"You know your own job, Captain. Thanks for dealing with this matter," Brentner told him, and he was about to depart when Rose Brentner appeared. There was a distinct gleam in her eyes which captivated Bony.

"What did you say, Captain?"

"That there'll be no more trouble, Missus."

"But before that you said something about a sliver of wood. What was that again?"

Her athletic figure was straight, and her brown eyes blazing. The aborigine stood firmly on his feet, and his voice was firm too. He said: "The usual penalty for a man and a woman running off together is a spear thrust under the woman's knee-cap, and a spear thrust in the back for the man. As Lawrence and Wandin were to be married black-feller fashion, a sliver of wood will keep both in camp a few weeks."

"I've never heard of such a thing," exclaimed Rose Brentner. "It shall not be. You will tell Gup-Gup and Poppa what I say. The very idea is abhorrent."

Captain stood his ground and glanced at Brentner for assistance. Tessa appeared behind Rose, and Rose asked if there was anything to prevent the shameless delinquents being married at once.

"The period of probation, Missus," replied Captain, and Tessa took him up on this point.

"There's no period of probation following the act of unlawful intercourse."

"Now we're getting all legal," complained Captain and again appealed to Brentner. Smiling appreciatively, Bony actually fumbled the making of a cigarette. He made his contribution: "Intercourse hasn't yet been proved."

The cattleman chuckled, and his wife tried to freeze him. Tessa was about to speak again and thought better of it.

"Well!" exclaimed Rose. "I live and learn, I must say. Captain you will stop the laming. At once. Tomorrow I'll talk to Gup-Gup and Poppa. Tell them so."

Yet again Captain wordlessly appealed to Brentner, and this time received his nod of acquiescence. The silence following his departure was terminated by Rose addressing her husband.

"Kurt, you weren't really going to allow that laming, were you?"

"Just politics, dear," Brentner said placatingly. "Away back in the Year One the abos passed an Act dealing with pre-marital and unlawful intercourse. The penalties for infringement were as you've just heard. The Ages alter little if anything. There's no difference between the blacks and us. An Act is defied by many voters, and it's then called a bad Act, and bad in law. Justice comes to be seen done, but isn't. Gup-Gup and Poppa know full well that to lame those two would mean I would have to report it and Howard would come out to investigate it."

"Are you sure? Poppa seemed very determined."

"Of course, I'm sure," her husband said. "In this case justice will be to be seen done, but won't be done. They'll lay those two on the ground, sharpen the slivers of wood, make a great song and dance about pretending to lame the criminals, and shut up about it. They don't want official interference any more than we want officialdom to interfere with them. Damn it, there's the gong and the sherry on the sideboard. Come on, everyone!"

After dinner, the two little girls invited Bony to inspect their school work, but once they got him to the school room they exhibited no interest in academic learning save along the path to aboriginal legends. Much amused by the diplomacy employed, Bony insisted on looking through and admiring their books and projects. When Tessa appeared she was complimented, and having gracefully accepted the praise, she consented to the children listening to legends for just one hour.

It was an hour long remembered by Bony. He sat at the table smoking his extraordinary cigarettes. The children sat opposite, and with paper and pencil the aboriginal girl made notes. He told one relating the adventures of the ancestor of the Urabunna who made a lot of gypsum which he tossed up into the sky, and which came down again in the form of rain and men and women. Which is why the Urabunna are called Rain Men. There is another which he related this evening concerning an ancestor of the Arunta Nation. In the Alchuringa a kangaroo named Ungutnika was afflicted with boils. He put up with these boils for a long time when, in anger, he pulled them out and threw them down and at once they became great boulders. And ever since, when a man wishes to afflict an enemy with boils, all he need do is to throw some toy spears at one of the stones, taking in evil magic, and then hurl them in the direction of the enemy.

Hilda wanted to know what a boil was and Tessa reminded her of a pimple she once had. Rosie thought she would make a toy spear and throw it against a large stone and then hurl it at Poppa who for some reason she disliked.

Bony persuaded each of them to tell him a legend, and, when Mrs. Brentner appeared to find out what was going on, Tessa was reminded of the time and Bony made a further request.

"Tell me the legend about the Crater, about Lucifer's Couch."

Little Rosie frowned, and Hilda appealed to Tessa.

"There isn't one about Lucifer's Couch," she said, putting down the pencil and gathering her notes. "I've never heard a legend about it, anyway."

"Too new, perhaps," offered Rose Brentner. "True legends have to take place in the Alchuringa, and be handed down and down . . . right into little girls' beds. Now, off with you. Say good night."

Hilda insisted on a good-night kiss, and Rosie claimed her right, and following them from the school room, Bony was invited to the lounge for coffee.

He could hear the cattleman talking over the transceiver in the office, and the subject was the coming visitation of the political tourists. In this Rose was not interested at the moment, her mind being directed to Tessa.

"She's been telling me about you, Bony. Told me of your early career at school and university. She said she mentioned her hobby of collecting legends, and also that she hopes to come home from Teachers College and teach here. What do you think of that idea? I mean about the College."

"She gave me the impression of being very keen about it, and I think you should send her down. Always provided you have a relative or friend to take care of her."

"Tessa would be staying with my sister. I'm not concerned on that point. I've been wondering, that if she goes down to College, will she be estranged from the aborigines here when she returns."

"That could be an advantage when she comes back to teach. You are very fond of her, are you not?"

"Very. The girl has a lovely disposition. About the College, though, there lingers in my mind a small doubt as to the wisdom of it. For a boy, yes, decidedly: but a girl . . ."

Bony did not press the matter, and Rose Brentner fell silent. They heard Kurt signing off, and a few minutes later he joined them.

"Well, what's the argument?" he asked. "Minister and party will arrive at Hall's in about three days. I told Leroy we'll be going in, and would pick him up if his wife wanted to stay home."

"I think she would like it if the children and I stayed with her while you and the men went in to town, don't you?"

"If you want it that way."

"Then I'll talk to her tomorrow evening."

"Good!"

"We've been discussing Tessa and the Teachers College," Rose said. "Bony thinks that if her absence somewhat estranges her from the Tribe it will be an advantage when she teaches here."

"About right, dear. Sometimes I think she's too close as it is. We must accept the fact that she's now a matured young woman. The call of instincts which are natural will sort of pull her more and more strongly toward her own people. Sending her away for three or four years will get her over a difficult period. Isn't that what you think, Bony?"

"It is what I think, yes," Bony admitted without hesitation. "The incident in the day-house earlier this evening gave support to what we seem to agree upon. Meaning what would be best for Tessa, although our approach to agreement would not follow the same line of reasoning."

Brentner and his wife stared hard: the man frowning, his wife evincing slight perturbation. Bony proceeded cautiously: "It has been nice of you both to accept me almost on a family basis. I know, of course, that you have a deep affection for Tessa. I know, too, that you are both ambitious for her and that you have sound reasons for being so. Thus anything which might hurt her would certainly hurt you.

"We said a moment ago that the girl had reached maturity and would feel ever stronger the pull of the Tribe, and that if she spent a few years away she would be strengthened when making her own decisions. You would not want her to marry a white man. Have you thought whom she might marry?"

"She could do much worse than marry Captain," Kurt asserted.

"Even better to marry an aboriginal parson or teacher," suggested his wife. "There's something on your mind, isn't there, Bony?"

"I've been wondering just how close Tessa is to her people. Has she given any sign of being in love with Captain, even being attracted to him?"

"Just the other way round, I think," replied Rose.

"Then what I am going to say, I will ask you to treat in strict confidence. There is a solution, I am sure, which we will eventually reach. Now, you will remember that Tessa did not contradict Captain's story of the man Lawrence running off with the girl he was about to marry. She did not contradict Captain when saying that Lawrence was at Eddy's Well for water, and was trapped at the shed by the appearance of Young Col and myself. Am I right?"

Both nodded agreement, and Bony offered his final point.

"It would seem that Tessa is much closer to the Tribe than you think. In the first place the girl, Wandin, is already married, and in the second place it wasn't Lawrence who ran from the well on being discovered."

11

THE COLLABORATORS

"I suppose you can support that extraordinary statement with proof," Rose Brentner said, and her husband spoke harshly, saying: "Of course he can. Go on, Bony. Let's have it."

"The girl bears between her breasts the chevron mark of the married woman," Bony informed them. "The neck of the nightdress thing she was wearing slipped open for a moment. I expect she was told to wear it in order to conceal the mark. The man with her behaved according to the situation. He was very nervous and he tried continually to dig his toes into the ground. The floor is hard. I noted that the smallest and the next toe of his left foot are missing. The aborigine at the Well had no such loss."

"Well I'm damned!" exclaimed the cattleman violently, and his wife sprang to Tessa's defence.

"But Tessa mightn't know that girl is married."

"Course she'd know, Rose. She visits her mother in the camp. She's not that much separated from them as not to know of a girl being married. Then the tale put up by Captain. What's your thinkin' on that point, Bony?"

"I'll take you further into my confidence because I believe you could and will go along with me. First: two facts. Before daylight the morning after I had ridden to the Crater, an abo had ridden a horse there and at first light tracked my horse and then me to the wall and over it to the floor. He rode the horse back to this homestead. I was out there and saw him, but not near enough to identify him. On my return to the homestead that morning I followed the Creek, and subsequently saw a lubra back-tracking me. Those facts speak for themselves.

"This morning when we met at breakfast no one knew I would be riding with Col to Eddy's Well. I didn't know it myself. The horses were in the yard, thirteen of them. Two were saddled for the ride to the Well, leaving eleven. You asked me to tell Col to tell Captain to have the eleven returned to the paddock. We came home through that paddock, and Young Col says that a horse named Star wasn't among them. We made sure Star wasn't inside the horse paddock.

"I'll go so far as to say I think it probable that after Young Col and I left this morning an aborigine rode Star to the Well with orders to arrive first and to watch what one or both of us did there. He would have to ride hard to arrive first. He probably tethered Star to a tree back in the grass. Now here is something of a flaw. When he cleared out on being discovered, he had time enough to ride Star back to the horse paddock before us. Why he failed in that, we shall know some day. The animal could have broken the tether. All this is supposition, but Star was not in the paddock when Col and I returned."

"All right!" Brentner said. "All right! You were tracked to the Crater. Why send a man to Eddy's Well to see what you did, when he could have gone there tomorrow and tracked what you did?"

"A good question without an answer at the moment. Another good question having no answer for us at the moment is why Captain and Poppa put up that cock-and-bull story about Lawrence and Wandin. One possible reason for the yarn was to impress on us that the aborigine we saw running away was one of two lovers. The truth is lacking, and no amount of bullying will extract the truth from the aborigines."

"We could get it out of Tessa. Go fetch her, Rose," snapped Brentner, his face reddened by anger.

"Wait!" Bony was sharply commanding. "That we must not do, because we may be doing Tessa an injustice. By acting circumspectly the answers to these provocative questions may be forthcoming tomorrow or the following day. I haven't confided to you these matters without consideration of a problem in which we three people are deeply interested. That is the preservation of the relationship of this tribe of aborigines with yourselves as representative of the white race. You wish that?"

"Of course we do. Go on," urged Brentner.

"You have often asked yourselves why the body was put on the floor of the Crater?"

"Often. Why put the body there at all beats me. There's a million acres of open country and a hundred million tons of dead wood to burn it to dust. Why? D'you know?"

"Yes, I think I do. I am convinced that it was put there by aborigines, yours or the wild men, possibly those at Beaudesert, with firm preference for your local tribe in view of their behaviour. Now don't jump to conclusions. I do not say, or believe as yet, that the man was killed by your local tribe. I do say your abos know who put the body there. Provided they did not kill and yet did put the body in the Crater, it might be managed to keep them out of the affair as being accessories. The authorities would not want to make a song and dance about them. Bad politics.

"Coming back to Tessa and Captain, we have the one dear to you and the other being of some importance in your lives. My assignment is to establish who killed that white man and how he arrived in this area without being reported. Until I am sure, I want to give your aborigines the benefit of the doubt that they killed him. And I want your collaboration."

For nearly a minute they considered this request, Rose steadily looking at her hands resting on her lap, Brentner staring at his shoes. It was Rose who agreed for both.

"How can we collaborate?" Brentner asked. "I'm feeling like being in my car with the wheels spinning and sinking into a bog."

"I've observed that every morning one of the aborigines walks out into the horse paddock which is a square mile in area and not very scrubby. He catches an old mare and rides after the other horses to bring them to the horse-yards at about seven. I'd like you to be at the yards, when the horses are brought there, and look Star over for evidence of hard riding. If the horse isn't there, have Young Col and Ted look for him and make sure he didn't get through the fence. If satisfied he didn't break through the fence, then make a great fuss about him and have riders out looking for him. Clear?"

"Yes, I'll do that."

"Without making Captain suspicious that you are particularly interested in that horse up to the moment it is missing from the paddock." Bony turned to Rose. "Now Mrs. Brentner, I have a most interesting assignment for you, and do hope you undertake it. You have slept badly by worrying over the threatened punishment of the lovers. So, first thing tomorrow you order Captain to report to you. You convince him you are most concerned about them, and you command him to take you at once to Gup-Gup. You will not be side-tracked. You will insist, stamping a foot to emphasise your determination, if necessary.

"Take Tessa with you. You will order Gup-Gup to marry the lovers at once, in your presence. You will insist. You will threaten discontinuance of the tobacco ration for the whole tribe if the lovers are not married in your presence.

You will observe his reactions and those of Poppa. They should be amusing because Gup-Gup will not dare to give a man's wife in marriage to a runaway lover. Thus we shall see how he wriggles to get out of that one."

"Gosh! That's a beauty," complimented the cattleman. "I'm all for it."

"And you, Mrs. Brentner?"

"Certainly, Bony. I find myself wanting to do that. I hate being deceived. I shall take Tessa with me, and she'll break my heart if she deceives me."

"Put on the racial cloak Tessa is wearing, Mrs. Brentner. Then you will learn that Tessa is battling against divided loyalty. It isn't a pleasant situation for anyone. I recall to your mind what she admitted when questioned why she ran off that day. Instinctively, she obeyed what she thought was right, and the same thing would have influenced her this evening when she did not openly challenge Captain's story of the lovers."

Rose looked directly into the blue eyes regarding her with the hint of appeal, and she knew in this moment that she would never understand Tessa as this man surely did, and the doubt vanished that he would act contrary to his professed approach to aborigines.

"To get back to Captain," said her husband. "I'm beat there. He cramps me for the first time. He's been brought up by white people, or near enough. He's been educated by white people. He reads and writes in a place of his own, and allowed to be pannikin boss who's trusted. He's nearly as far removed from the Tribe as Tessa. If what we think is correct, then he's just a double-crossing black bastard. The days of ill-treating a black are long past, but I've a mind to thrash it out of him."

"You know quite well, Kurt, that nothing is gained by thrashing an aborigine. You know, too, it would bring unhappiness to many people, including yourselves," countered Bony with calmness surprising Rose Brentner. "Action springs from motive. We do not know the motive resulting in the death of the Crater man. We do know, or may think we know with confidence, that his murder was not actuated by greed. I said just now that Tessa was probably struggling against divided loyalty. It could be so with Captain. Therefore, charity and not condemnation shall be the motive actuating us tomorrow. I'll employ a few clichés. We mustn't rush our fences or charge about like a bull in a china shop. Everything will come out in the wash."

"I adore clichés," Rose avowed unsmilingly. "Kurt, you behave. We have agreed to do certain things first thing in the morning. They will be more interesting than losing the temper and thrashing an aborigine. You look for that horse. Leave Captain and Gup-Gup to me."

The powerful, square-faced cattleman who had thrived on battling with drought and flood and fire, who had fisted his way to and fro across these northern mountains and over the spaces of the arid desert, subsided physically and mentally, and grinned like a boy found in an apple tree.

"The wife's always right," he admitted to Bony. "We start a race. I ride straight and true and hard. She rides round corners, stops to admire the scenery, rides on again and stops to do her hair. And gets first to the post. It's been always like that."

"Well, it isn't hard to take, is it?" asked the chuckling Bony.

"No, not particularly."

"And you should agree that Bony is right, too, Kurt," added his wife using the other spur. Smiling, she turned to Bony. "And what will you be doing first thing in the morning?"

"Watching the sunrise. Employing my mighty intellect.

Meanwhile you might manage to steal from the larder a few biscuits and a piece of cheese, a little tea and sugar and a quart pot to brew tea. And you, Kurt, could loan a pistol as I seem always to leave mine at home."

On retiring to his room, Bony was equipped for his expedition to see the sun rise, and at one o'clock he left the house by his bedroom window and slipped away from the homestead without rousing the dogs.

Although the night was moonless he had to accept the risk of being observed by the glow of the meteors which appear to be singularly attracted by this Kimberley Country.

Walking at night across a desert, which isn't as denuded of herbage as the Sahara, is something else to walking a city street during a blackout. Here it was necessary to avoid the spinifix, the small areas of porcupine grass, the low bush and taller scrub trees, all traps to cause halt or floundering and all obstacles to catch and imprison wisps of wool from his ungainly wool shoes. Bony needed his good eyesight to avoid the traps and keep to the open sandy spaces. Direction was instinctive, and to follow a course required no thought.

The feeling of isolation in space without limits was, however, strong. There were no landmarks to provide knowledge of movement, no lift or depression anywhere on the circular horizon determined only by the edge of black under the lighter tint of the sky. It was not unlike walking in fog rising to the waist. In the fog lurked the obstructions to be avoided, and the open sandy areas to be crossed without hindrance. Race instincts plus inherited gifts enabled this man to cross the desert as though in daylight.

There was no wind. The night was silent, void of sound. Bony created no sound, not even the tiny sound of feet crunching sand that occurs when a man is wearing boots.

Once he fell into a dry water-gutter, its edges steep after the last flooding, the floor three feet below the surface.

Shortly after this shaking he fancied he saw immediately to the front a moving object. He halted, sniffed the air without result, listened to the soft crunch of sand and heard nothing. Stooping, he sought to bring the object against the sky, and found this not to be done. Upright again, he thrust his right hand into the side pocket of his tunic and brought out the automatic. The object was there, without doubt. He could sense its proximity. If it would move again . . . A meteor flamed. Six feet from him a large kangaroo was balanced back against its tail, its powerful forearms extended to grip when one of its hind legs could disembowel a man with a foot.

Both man and animal were startled. Bony stepped aside, and the kangaroo went to ground and fled even as the meteor expired.

An hour later a cool zephyr fanned Bony's cheek and brought with it the smell of cattle camped till the dawn. He had passed them when the lowing of a cow gave their position. The false dawn came to warn him, and when the genuine dawn flared high into the eastern sky he came to the mill and water tanks of Eddy's Well. Long before sunrise he was concealed in the tall buffalo grass where the naked aborigine had vanished.

12

THE MORTICIANS

Like a partridge on her nest eggs, Bony sat in the buffalo grass with his back to a tree. To his front the grass provided a thin screen permitting clear sight of Eddy's Well. The sun was gleaming on the mill vanes being slowly agitated by the early morning wind which, he hoped, would not become strong and sing too loudly in the grass and so blanket other and more sinister sounds.

Although not complacent, he was confident he had left no tracks throughout the night journey save where he had fallen into the water-gutter, and as that was about four miles from the homestead it was unlikely to be observed by an aborigine. He was satisfied by the plans he had made to mask his absence from the homestead and that at this moment Rose Brentner would have begun her act with Captain, demanding to be escorted to Gup-Gup and Company without delay. Captain would be so enmeshed in these contretemps to his story of illicit romance that no thought of Bony would occur, and it could well be midday before he realised that Bony was off stage.

Upon Captain's troubled waters would blow the wind of Brentner's interest in his working horses, further to unseat Captain's normal equilibrium and make his morning a period of confusion in which the activities of the detective could have no place. Bony's problem was to find the answer to the question Kurt Brentner had asked: Why send in haste a spy to Eddy's Well to see what he did when the same spy or another could without risk of discovery find that out by tracking his horse. A possible answer barely logical was that the spy had been sent to overhear what was spoken at the lunch fire, his position behind the shed enabling him to do so.

Bony thought it could reasonably be presumed that in this Eddy's Well area there was something of great importance to the station aborigines which it was desired he should not stumble upon, but what this could be would never become known while he, Bony, sat in the grass like a partridge on her nest.

His position was at the southern edge of a delta-shaped area of water-courses, small lakes, amid desert gums and grass, the whole flooded when Deep Creek ran for a week, as previously told by Young Col. Now every yard of it was bone dry, covered with grass as high as a man, and through it the pads made by cattle to reach the Well. It was no place for woollen shoes, and these he had changed for his riding boots.

He climbed the tree, seeing then the skirting desert narrowing toward the north and enclosing grass and trees like a grey carpet speckled with green and brown. What could possibly be amid this dry, desolate, depressing, grass-delta he was not to discover unknown to the station aborigines? It could have no connection with the murder on Lucifer's Couch. It could be associated with the history, the rites, the ceremonies of the local Tribe, because in the far past this area would have been permanently covered with water and the home of wild fowl, and so the origin of many legends of great importance.

He was about to descend to the ground when a crow found him, cawed while whirling about his tree, and it became obvious that the bird had had a prior interest, when, venting protest at the unknown thing in the tree, it flew on over the grass land to settle in another where it was joined by others whose cawing spoke of resentment at being disturbed. Knowing bird language is ever a help, and having listened to it for thirty seconds Bony decided that the conference wasn't about animated beings.

The horse lay on a cattle pad or trail through the grass. Its position proved that it had been headed for the Well when death overtook it. On the forehead was a white star. The open mouth, the remains of the protruding tongue, the crusty white sweat marks on the coat combined to prove that the unfortunate animal had been ridden bareback until it collapsed from exhaustion. The rider had removed the bridle.

That it had been dead less than twenty-four hours was plainly evident, and that it was the station horse named Star Bony was sure. From the edge of the grass he could see the mark ahead of the carcase made by the rider when he crashed to ground on the trail. The story was clear: the sequel could come at any moment.

Slipping back into the grass, he selected a tree which he climbed and gained position giving him sight of the carcase, and here he waited and pondered upon the likely developments. The horse had been taken and ridden by the spy until it collapsed. The man had been thrown heavily. He had run on to the Well to fulfil his mission. Discovery had sent him back to walk the fifteen miles to the homestead where he would arrive long after the horsemen. The time could be shortly after five o'clock.

At five o'clock Captain would know about the aborigine seen at the Well. He would know something serious had happened to the spy, and probably he was in conference with Gup-Gup when the man showed up to report the death of the horse. Discovery of the carcase would be very serious to the Tribe in general and himself in particular, no matter when it was discovered, because no manufactured theory could be made to square with the estimated time of death, the location and the position of the carcase. It would have to be taken care of at once.

At dawn, this day Bony was concealed in a tree, a party of aborigines would leave the station camp. Not before dawn because they hate being abroad during dark nights. Travelling fast, it would occupy four hours, and the termination of the fourth hour was now. Meanwhile Captain would be engaged with the determined Rose Brentner with Gup-Gup squirming on his hook, and by this time her husband would be "going to market" about his absent horse. No one at the homestead would be wondering why Inspector Bonaparte was so late for breakfast.

The crows had settled again after he left the carcase, and it was fully thirty minutes later when they rose in renewed uproar. Bony was thankful for the time lapse, because when they rose at his arrival they would not have been observed by the party now materialising to gather about the dead horse.

There were eighteen men under the command of Poppa, and Bony wondered how they would solve their problem of disposing of the body. To burn it would be to leave a large area of ash. To convey it to another place would be no solution. To dump it into Lucifer's Couch would be absurd. To take it to another place and bury it might prove disastrous as the wild dogs would surely burrow down to it and the crows would wait for their leavings and thus draw attention. There was one solution: to dig a deep pit, but they had no shovels and they had no lubras to dig a hole with digging sticks. It would mean much hard work, anyway.

That they had brought knives indicated planning. They removed the forelegs with the shoulders. They removed the hind legs at the hips. That left the dismembered body intact, and with very little blood letting. They had brought poles with them, and they used the poles as stretchers to carry away the remains, leaving Poppa and another to remove all evidence remaining on the ground.

The Medicine Man and his assistant went off after the bearers, and the angry and frustrated crows revealed the way taken by the morticians. They were following the trail deeper into the grass land.

Bony gave them twenty minutes before following along this same trail, with the grass either side often higher than himself and the trail continuously winding and presenting angles he had to prospect with care. The tracks made by the party were plain on the dusty surface of the trail, and the crows were allies telling him how far ahead were the bearers.

He halted to listen when men shouted, proceeding when the shouting ceased. Minutes later, on rounding a corner, he came face to face with a bull, and before the bull could recover from the encounter, he stepped into the grass and waited there while a long line of cattle passed on their way to the Well. The aborigines had driven a mob onto the trail to obliterate their own tracks and make certain that the scene of the equine tragedy was also obliterated.

The cattle having passed, Bony kept to the grass, walking parallel with the trail, eventually coming to the place where the beasts had been driven to take it. Later on he peered for the hundredth time round a bend before proceeding and saw Poppa and his assistant beating out the tracks with leafy tree branches. Still later, he saw ahead above the grass an oddity: sharply rising ground the colour of the great desert.

On drawing closer he could distinguish the small stones covering what appeared to be a blunt desert finger stabbing at the heart of the grass land, and then he witnessed the undertakers struggling up to the summit with their burdens. Arrived there, they set the poles down, and began an operation the reason for which he could not observe. This accomplished, they returned to the poles, lifted them and appeared to upend them. Thereafter, they looked as though gathering rocks and stones and depositing them at a central point.

Eventually the activity ceased, and the party moved back along the desert finger for several hundred yards where could be seen above the general level the topmost branches of several baobab trees. Here they disappeared for ten or fifteen minutes, and on coming again into Bony's vision they walked back to the tip of the finger, descended to the grass and vanished. They were not carrying anything Bony could detect. The thwarted crows settled among the baobabs.

Bony settled, too, in the grass and, as the light wind was coming from the north, made and lit a cigarette. The aborigines had, with little doubt, begun the journey back to the camp, and he was fully convinced of it when three miles toward the homestead there rose a column of disjointed smoke, the wind making it useless as a message save perhaps to announce a fact, the fact that the job was done announced to a waiting watcher at the camp.

Bony permitted an hour to pass before he walked to the place where the poles had been upended. The poles were not there. They and the remains of the horse had been tossed into a long-abandoned prospector's mine shaft, and after the remains had been tossed stones and rock splinters from the mullock raised when mining.

Mentally complimenting Poppa, he proceeded to the baobab trees, and discovered that they grew in a deep basin of upthrust granite and areas of surface rock showing on the floor of sand. There were five baobabs, ancient, enormous in girth, scarred by time, their branches gnarled, the leaves isolated one from the others, seemingly monstrous relics still living after half a million years of borrowed time. Compared with the young and graceful baobabs on the mountain gullies, these were almost obscene.

The sand areas were clean of tracks. On a wide slab of surface rock remained some of the ash from a large fire. On other surface rocks was similar ash, denoting much smaller fires. Almost in the centre of the basin the ashes of a small fire gave off wisps of smoke.

This, Bony was convinced, was the Tribe's Initiation Camp. The major fire would be the Corroboree Fire, and the smaller sites would have been the fires over which the men held secret converse. The possible reason why Poppa and his companions had come here after disposing of the horse was for water. It was also likely that somewhere here would be the Tribe's Treasure House where is kept the most powerful churingas, the pointing bones, and the magic red and yellow ochres. If he could find that, he would indeed be powerful.

The still hot fire on the sand claimed his interest. Why had the aborigines made it there? They hadn't been that long out of his sight to cook anything. He had heard of such being a decoy in reverse, and with a thick stick he moved the ash aside and began to delve with his hands, scooping the sand from the hole he made, widening the hole and so going down for a dozen or fifteen inches when he came upon a sheet of stiff and hard hide.

Lifting this out with care, there was disclosed lying on a second sheet the pointing bones, a dozen carved churinga stones, cutting flints, lumps of gypsum, and a tiny ivory Buddha.

13

BUDDHA AND MISTER LAMB

Kneeling at the edge of the excavation, gazing at the instruments of magic, good and evil, it seemed to the man of two races that the world about him was hushed by his act of sacrilege. The silence became a weight pressing against his ears, and the aborigine in him struggled to banish the other half of his personality.

He was to remember that it was the ivory Buddha which provided the jolt of surprise enabling him to retain the equilibrium which was sometimes threatened. The Buddha represented a foreign culture, and its presence so demanded an explanation that the other articles lost their sinister effect on him.

The sheet of bark was a bed of red and white bird feathers glued with tree resin, and on this beside the many cutting flints and lumps of gypsum lay the full set of pointing bones and several spear heads also used as pointing instruments. The boning set consisted of five needle-pointed thin bones taken from kangaroos. Six to seven inches in length, the butts were attached to human hair string with tree gum, one of the bones at the end of the string being that actually pointed at the victim. To the other end of the string was a pair of eagle's claws, and similarly attached by hair to the main string was a hair net containing what would be a powerful churinga stone full of magic.

The spear heads, and the large flints, had a short hair string attached, and at the other end of the string was the accompanying churinga in its hair net. These could be used more secretly by one man, whereas the complicated set of bones often required two to operate. Bony recalled when he was boned, feeling the grip of eagles' claws wrenching at his liver and kidneys, and it was with extreme distaste that he lifted the collection on the hide and then found the purpose of the aborigines' visit.

There was disclosed a floor of rock, and across the floor a two-inch crack. On a splinter of rock being dropped, Bony heard it splash on water. With a grass stem a man could suck water from the reservoir, and Poppa having removed his instruments without permitting his companions to see them, each man had been able to refresh himself for the journey back to camp.

Bony carefully replaced the tray and covered it with the top sheet of hide, then with haste filled in the excavation and lit a small fire on the site to leave it exactly as found. When again in the grass and having a tree for a back rest, he chain smoked and sought for a possible explanation of the presence of the Buddha with the pointing bones.

It was about two inches long and slightly less in width. Through the head, from ear to ear a hole was bored to take a string or very fine gold chain, probably to be suspended from the neck as a charm or talisman. That it had some significance in Poppa's Cache of Magic could not be doubted, and the obvious answer was that a lugger crewman at Broome, or another port, had traded it with a coast aborigine. This man had in turn traded with an inland aborigine, and it could have followed one of the mysterious trade routes to come into Poppa's possession, gathering power when being "sung" all along the way.

The Aboriginal Culture is like a well to the bottom of

which no white man has ever descended to the water of complete knowledge, and because of the ever-expanding influence of an alien white race, no white man ever will. Confusion has been created by the white man himself to add to the certainty of frustration and defeat in his latter day efforts to investigate. Today it isn't possible to determine what are the legitimate legends and what the fabrications of imaginative white men.

The obvious about anything associated with aborigines cannot be trusted, and Bony had advanced no further when, having slept till evening, he left the grass on the return to the homestead. It was shortly after the dawn that he appeared at the kitchen seeking a pannikin of tea, arrayed in a maroon gown, blue slippers, and carrying a toilet bag and towel.

"Mornin', Inspector Bonaparte! How you coming?" was the cook's greeting.

"I'm hoping there's left a pannikin of your first tea," replied the cheerful Bony.

"There's never no hope, never at all. The kettle's boiling. Empty the pot of leaves and make some more. I'm perishing. Where you been?"

"Went over to the Beaudesert people to have a yarn, Jim. Have you been behaving yourself while I was away?"

"Me! I wouldn't know how," answered the cook. "But the Boss's been going crook, and the Missus went to market down at the Black's Camp. And that sort of upset Mister Lamb who went and disgraced himself something terrible."

"H'm!" With impatience Bony waited for the tea to brew. "Just as well I gave myself a walking holiday. What did Mister Lamb do?"

"He went and mis-cued."

"He did what?"

Scolloti deftly dropped the last portion of smooth dough

into the last of the greased tins, and wiped his floured hands on a rag. Then portentously he sat at the table, saying: "Pour us a pannikin, Inspector. I never been drunk on tea: wish I could. Yes, after all these years of un-blemished record Mister Lamb mis-cued. It was yesterday morning. It was so bad I could of yowled tears of blood. He missed the pocket by a couple of yards."

"You don't say," murmured Bony, helping himself to a sweet scone. "Two yards! That does sound bad. How did it happen?"

"Don't know how it happened. It did happen. Of course Mister Lamb could have been upset by the Boss roarin' and screamin' over at the yards 'cos one of the horses is missing. Anything what upsets the peace like, upsets Mis-ter Lamb. Then he goes off with the Missus and Tessa to the Blacks' Camp, and I seen him coming back by him-self and looking determined like he'd made up his mind never to leave home again. He came to the door and winged for a bit of tobacco, and I give him a shred or two and he went off to lie in the sun at yonder tree.

"Well, the next thing is there's a hell of a thud against the outside wall. Someone yells, and then there's a few real live curses. Mind you, I'm sitting right here where I am now, and I'm wondering what all this is about when in comes Toby. He looks like the laundry lubras has passed him through the mangle, but this can't be as it isn't wash-ing day. Toby's nose is bleeding bad, and he's favoring his left arm and his right leg. I asks him what he wants, and he sits down and starts bleeding over the floor. And then when Mister Lamb looks in through the door I still don't cotton that he mis-cued."

"It would be hard to accept," Bony gravely agreed. "Who is this Toby?"

"One of the blacks. Works now and then mustering. Now there he is bleeding like a stuck pig and me worried to death about Mister Lamb. I got a hunk of rag and give it to Toby, and I went out to see if anyone had seen what happened. Luckily no one was about, and I come in and found Toby's nose has stopped bleeding. It was sort of serious, you see, 'cos the Boss had threatened to get rid of Mister Lamb once he done harm to anyone, and Toby looked harmed all right.

"Anyway, I took Toby out at the back and made him shove his head into a bucket of water, and that didn't do him no extra harm. He tells me it was Mister Lamb what done it. He said he forgot about Mister Lamb as he had brought a note for me from the Missus. He's a real wild abo too. So I brought him in again and gives him a pannikin of tea and a whole jam tart I had to hand. I was still trying hard to convince him it wasn't Mister Lamb what flung him against the wall, and that he must have tripped or something, when in comes the two kids and Hilda let out it was Mister Lamb and that they had seen him mis-cue."

"Both reliable witnesses, Jim. Of course you continued to defend Mister Lamb?"

"Well, what do you think? He's the only humorist about the place. Anyway, the kids say they were working at their lessons in the school room when it happened, and I sits them down at the table and give 'em hot jam roll I just took from the oven to sweeten 'em up. I tells them and Toby that we'd be lost without Mister Lamb around, and that we'd all better forget what happened; say nothing to no one; keep it dark as it was the first mis-cue ever since Captain had passed him as champion.

"The kids was willing, and, after they done a bit of coaxing, Toby found his arm was all right and his leg wasn't broke, and a quarter-pound plug of tobacco pushed under his nose, and he agreed Mister Lamb didn't mean to ram him through the wall instead of through the door-way."

Bony badly wanted to laugh at the manner of the telling rather than the hurtful result of Mister Lamb's behaviour, and gained the victory because Scolloti was deadly serious.

"So you were able to make the incident a homestead secret," he said, pouring himself a second pannikin of tea. "What happened to the note Toby brought from Mrs. Brentner? Was that lost?"

"No. I got that all right. It was only to give Toby the Bible on the shelf in the day room."

"Oh!" Bony inwardly chuckled. "And the missing horse hasn't been located, you said."

"Something wrong somewhere," Jim said, glancing at his clock. "Horses don't go and clear out all by theirselves. The Boss is going dead crook. Gonna have every man out today looking for it. Well, it's me for the breakfast to start 'em."

Bony intentionally delayed appearing for breakfast until Brentner and the men had left on the muster, and he joined Rose and the children with Tessa shortly after they sat down. Rosie wanted to know where he had gone on his walkabout.

"Almost to Beaudesert. Not quite, as I dawdled at the Crater too long. How have you two been getting along? I remembered a couple of legends and I'll tell them after lunch." Tessa served his breakfast and resumed her seat which happened to be opposite his own. She was wearing a white blouse above a black pleated skirt, and her hair this morning was drawn back which gave her round face the look of severity which didn't belong. Hilda was rebelling against eating her cereal.

"I think I'll tell one of the legends," Bony said. "Ready? Well, there was an old lubra who had so many hungry little children she didn't know what to do. The kangas were scarce, and the men had no food to spare. So she took the children off hunting for something to eat, and they went a long, long way and found nothing. After a while they came to a big baobab tree growing all alone, and they all sat down and began sucking their thumbs just for something to make them forget how hungry they were. Then the baobab tree said: 'If you look . . .'"

Bony proceeded to eat, and with her spoon hovering over her untouched plate, Hilda waited with expectant eyes for him to continue. He appeared to have forgotten about the legend. Tessa told the child to get on with her breakfast as school would be punctual this morning, and Rosie urged him to tell what the Baobab said.

"What the Baobab said? Oh! Eat up, Hilda. No, that wasn't what the Baobab Tree said. It is what I said. No it's not. It's what . . . There you are making me all confused. Do get on with your breakfast, Hilda, so I can finish the legend. That's right. Well the Baobab said: 'If you look into my larder you'll find a lot of nardoo seeds you can grind into flour for porridge, and there's something else too. There's two legs and two shoulders of beef hanging up on a hook. So you all cut off steaks and make a fire and cook them, and I promise you will never be hungry again.'"

Hilda finished her portion of porridge, taking second place with him. Her eyes were bright, and rebellion forgotten.

"Well, the children and the old lubra looked for the Baobab's larder. They had to climb up the ugly old trunk to the big entrance at the top. Then they had to make a rope and lower one of the boys down inside to where the larder was, there being no steps or anything. Well, when the hungry little boy was lowered right down he began to cut steaks off the beef and eat them raw, and when he had stuffed himself he was too heavy to be pulled up, and too tired to cut off any more steaks to be pulled up by the rope.

"So they lowered a little girl down to the larder, and she cut off steaks and stuffed and stuffed without any thought of the others up top whose mouths were watering. Then she was so heavy they couldn't pull her up, and another little boy was lowered. And so it went on until only the poor old lubra was left on top of the trunk. You can imagine what she felt like, eh?"

"What?" pressed Rosie, and her sister echoed the question. Rose Brentner was gently smiling, and Tessa was regarding Bony with large and solemn black eyes.

"Well there she was, as hungry as a, as a bandicoot. So she tied the end of the rope to a branch and began to lower herself down inside the trunk. Then the rope broke and she fell to the bottom among all the little boys and girls who were so full they couldn't move. The old lubra took up the knife and cut steaks and ate them raw, and the funny thing was that the legs and shoulders of beef never became smaller. What a feast they had, to be sure. Eat, eat, and eat, and the larder never growing empty."

"How did they all get out in the end, Inspector?" queried Rosie, and Hilda added: "Yes, how?"

"They never did get out," answered Bony, casting a fleeting glance at Tessa. "The rope broke high up, and they couldn't mend it and so climb out. And ever since when anyone passes under that tree the Baobab says in a loud voice: 'Climb up and see what is in my larder.' But no one ever does, because anyone would know that baobab trees don't have larders."

Hilda placed her fairy-like hand on Bony's wrist and said, appealingly: "Thank you. Now tell us the other legend, please."

"Not till after school," decided her mother. "And not

then if Inspector Bonaparte is busy. I'll tell you what, though. The main lesson this morning could be writing an essay about that lovely legend. What do you think, Tessa?"

"It will be fine. We haven't had an essay for days," replied Tessa.

"But what shall we call the old lubra?" asked Rosie, and Bony said: "Well, she wasn't so very old, you know. Only old to the children, that's all. Let's call her Irititisatassa. You could make it shorter, of course. You could call her Tessa."

Tessa laughed with the children, and when she had taken them off for morning school, Rose Brentner fell to studying Bony when asking would he care for another cup of coffee.

14

KEEN ON LEGENDS

Changing position to sit closer to his hostess, Bony asked: "How did the wedding go off?"

"It did not go off," Rose replied. "It was a fiasco. Just where have you been during all the uproar?"

"Learning legends from baobab trees. Some are full of legends. What is your husband doing today?"

"They're all going looking for the horse. It wasn't in the paddock yesterday morning. Kurt is really angry about it. It's not the value of the horse that stirred him, but conviction that an aborigine took it. He's organised the two boys and half a dozen black stockmen, including Captain, to muster. Would you know anything of it?"

"I am more interested in the wedding you say did not take place."

"Well, with Captain and Tessa, I went to see Gup-Gup. When we arrived at the camp, Gup-Gup was asleep in his wurley. I had Captain fetch him out. I made Captain bring a box for me to sit on, and Gup-Gup who was wearing an old army overcoat squatted before me. There was nothing of the magnificent savage about him. Just a nasty dirty-looking old man. He mumbled something to a lubra, and she brought four other nasty dirty-looking old men who squatted behind him. Thank you."

Bony extinguished the match he had held in service, and made no comment. Rose went on: "I began by asking what had been done to Lawrence and the girl, and Gup-Gup said in effect that nothing had been done to them as I had told Captain they hadn't to be harmed. Then he said, and he wasn't insolent: 'Missus tell Captain that abo laws no good any longer. So nothing done to Wandin and Lawrence for breaking abo laws.'

"I then demanded that they be brought, and by this time there's a dozen lubras and all the children by the look of it, and more of the men. Captain spoke in their tongue, and the men began to shout, and soon Lawrence came and then the girl. I noticed they walked all right, and then I said that as they were to be married, they must be married right now. I thought I was smart, and I told them that as they had broken the law, the sooner they were married proper black-feller fashion the sooner the abo law would be repaired. That is what you wanted me to do, isn't it?"

"Yes. What happened then?"

"It was as you anticipated. The old men began to mumble among themselves. Gup-Gup drew pictures on the ground with a stick. The women were silent, and a middle-aged aborigine I don't remember ever having seen then began to shout at Gup-Gup who didn't take any notice of him. Captain shouted something and the strange aborigine stopped his noise. I thought . . . Would he be Wandin's husband, d'you think?"

"Quite likely," replied Bony. "As the girl's rightful husband, he would naturally protest at her marriage with Lawrence. What is he to look at?"

"Oh! I'd say he was taller than the average. Very powerful. He had two front teeth missing. There was an open cut down his forehead on the right side. Tessa said his name is Mitti. She told me that on the way home. The old men went on muttering; Gup-Gup went on drawing with his stick. No one seemed to get anywhere, and I was determined I'd sit there all day and wear them out."

"You might sit for eternity and not wear them out," Bony said.

"That's what I began to feel about it all. And so I told them if they wouldn't marry the lovers then I would, and I ordered a young aborigine to come to me. It just happened I had in my pocket an envelope, and Tessa had a pencil. So I wrote a note to Jim Scolloti asking him to give Toby, the young aborigine I'd called, a Bible for Toby to bring back at once. Then I read the note aloud, and told Toby to hurry, and to Gup-Gup I said I'd marry them myself.

"This started the fellow with a gash on his forehead shouting something I couldn't understand, and Tessa said he was protesting about the tribal laws being broken one after another. Toby was away a long time, and when he came with the Bible he looked as though he'd been in a fight. I questioned him about it, and he said he'd tripped over a root and hurt his face. And then when I had the Bible and was going to make pretend to marry the couple, they had vanished. They weren't there, that's all."

"Didn't Tessa see which way they went? Where?" pressed Bony, his eyes gleaming with humour.

"She said not. Are you laughing because I was waiting at the church, waiting at the church?"

"Partly. What happened to the tall abo with the wounded face?"

"The man who protested so violently? I don't remember. I think he vanished too."

"And Poppa, the Medicine Man?"

"I didn't see him at all."

"Then what did you do? After the lovers vanished?"

"I told them through Captain there would be no more tobacco issue until the lovers were properly married in my presence." Rose Brentner's mood lifted. "I doubt I could have married them, anyway. There's a Prayer Book, somewhere, but I couldn't think where it was. Did I do all right?"

"Splendidly. You are now convinced that the lady is the wife of Mitti?" Rose said it certainly appeared to be so, and Bony drummed his fingers on the tablecloth as he reviewed the picture she had drawn for him.

"What does it all mean?" she asked, trying to penetrate the veil worn by Gup-Gup and the others. Her failure made her petulant.

"There is an axiom which in effect says if your opponent lies in the sun all day you can do nothing with him. When I came here I found everyone metaphorically lying in the sun. It was necessary to prod everyone into activity. Well, now everyone is active. There's Gup-Gup wriggling on your hook. You haven't said much about Captain, but he will be a much worried man. Mitti, the fellow with the wounded head, is dancing with jealous rage; and without doubt Poppa will be cooking up some counter to explain the vanished horse. From all the activity will emerge, I hope, the solution of the Lucifer's Couch mystery. You mentioned that Tessa interpreted what Mitti said as a protest against abo laws being broken. Was that on your way home?"

"Yes, it was."

"It was then firmly in your mind that the protest was against marriage to Lawrence of the woman belonging to Mitti?"

"Yes. You see, I couldn't understand a word, but he kept on pointing to her and then to himself. She was certainly frightened, and once he gripped her wrist and held her for several minutes."

"And yet Tessa interpreted, afterwards, that Mitti protested against broken laws. Who would be right: Tessa or you?"

Rose closed her eyes as though they pained her, and when she looked again at him they emitted anger.

"Sometimes, Inspector Bonaparte, you are exasperating. I had my mind lock away the doubt of Tessa, and you drag it forth. I admit that I know the man was protesting against Wandin being married to Lawrence. Even Lawrence was frightened by what he said. What can we do about Tessa?"

"Why, nothing at all. She is only serving two masters without realising it. When she does, she'll decide for one or the other. By the way, have you ever seen a tiny ivory Buddha worn as a charm or talisman?"

"A Buddha! How you do prod people. No, I cannot say I have."

"I am glad to hear you say that." Bony gazed thoughtfully at his fingers rolling a cigarette, and, waiting for the next prod, Rose noted the well-groomed hair and profile of this man who could have modelled for a magazine illustrator.

"Did you arrange with Mrs. Leroy to stay with her while Kurt was at Hall's Creek?" he asked.

"Ethel Leroy appreciated the offer, and would not hear of it. Said I was to go to Hall's and take the children as it would be a real break for all of us. Her sister will be staying with her."

"And you're going?"

"I hope so. Kurt was too furious this morning to talk about it."

"And if he agrees you will go . . . when?"

"It will have to be tomorrow. Will you be coming with us?"

"I think not, but you could save me a possible trip to

seek information from Mrs. Leroy. I'll remind you of the matter before you leave. It concerns legends."

"Legends! You seem particularly keen on legends. Are you writing a book about them?"

"I might when I have completed this assignment." He laughed at himself. "The subject is of profound interest to wandering anthropologists, and all the local legends should be preserved before the Gup-Gups pass on. To return to the trip. You would like to go?"

"Oh yes. It is a break, you know. Besides there will be a lot of other women there to gossip with. And children too. Often I feel we are unduly isolated."

"Then I shall insist on your husband taking you. In return, will you support me when the time comes?"

Rose Brentner laughed openly, saying she could not believe he needed supporting at any time, but would do so. Then she said she had chores to do, and he left her and wandered across to the kitchen.

"I been thinking about you," the cook said, his dark and piercing eyes distinctly troubled. "You didn't say anything about Mister Lamb mis-cueing, did you?"

"Of course not," Bony assured him. "I like Mister Lamb, and owe him no grudge. In fact, I've just given him the best cigarette I've made for a month. Have you found out why he mis-cued?"

Scolloti pulled his ragged beard and sighed, saying: "Don't get it. The worry is that if he mis-cues again someone is going to see it, and then the Boss is going to send him back where he come from when a real lamb. It ain't natural for him to mis-cue like that. Could of done Toby a bit of harm, couldn't he?"

"Could have? I thought you said he did."

"That was nothing. No arms and legs broke. If the Boss heard it, him being in the rage he was yesterday and this morning, it'd be the partin' of the ways for Mister Lamb and the kids. He got real sore at the blacks, includin' Captain, about Star. Swore that one of 'em pinched the horse to go chasin' after a lubra over at the Leroy's. Told Captain it's high time he got himself a lubra, anyhow, instead of moonin' around like a sick eunuch. Sore! Cripes, he was sore."

"Captain hasn't a lubra, then?"

"Never did have as far as I know. Had a couple of tries at Tessa but was knocked back. She's a clever little wench that one. You don't know what goes on inside her. They say education ruins the blacks, but I reckon nothing can ruin 'em more than they are. As for Captain, well it ain't natural for a black to live in a place by himself and do nothin' at night bar read poetry."

"Is that what he does?"

"That and books on history. Gets 'em from the Missus. She gets 'em up from Perth. Why, he can write a better fist than me."

"I suppose that's where he gets his legends to tell the children?" probed Bony, made happy by the trend of this conversation.

"Must of. He tells 'em legends I've never heard of, and I've heard a lot in me time. You gets the chance to hear 'em when camped with a mustering team."

"Did you ever hear a legend about how the Crater was made?"

"No, can't say that I ever did. But then there wouldn't be no legends about that. It happened a long time after the blacks started legends."

"Some say the meteor fell about six hundred years ago."

"Well, I can say it fell in 1905. In January of that year. There's people who saw it fall, plenty of 'em. And heard it too. There wasn't anyone living out here then, of course, 'cept the wild blacks, and they was wild in them days. There was Joe the Stinker and his mate prospectin' for gold in the mountains a bit east of Hall's. They'd camped in their tent, and the light lit it all up and they went out, saw it fall, and heard the roar of it. If it fell six hundred years back instead of less'n sixty there'd be blacks' legends about it all right."

"The wild blacks would dream them up?"

"Too right they would. 'Course, Captain could make 'em, but he's the odd bloke out."

15

ANOTHER BOUT WITH GUP-GUP

Gup-Gup sat on an empty sack beside his small fire, the tenuous smoke from which drifted slantingly to miss the head of Poppa. The lubras and the children were less vociferous this afternoon than was usual.

Now and then Gup-Gup vented a soft grunt, and Poppa's eyes would flash in anger. They had been thus engaged for an hour without uttering a word when the tip of a shadow passed between them and there was the white-feller policeman looking down at them.

"The son of Illiwalli first blinds those he seeks," muttered the Chief. "One time it would not be so."

"One time a stranger would sign to enter a camp," growled Poppa.

"One time all abos not such fools," countered Bony before squatting on his heels and reaching for tobacco and papers.

They watched him, his face and fingers alternately, watched him replace the tin of tobacco and the papers and light the cigarette. Neither spoke again, and the minutes piled to total twenty when Poppa lost the duel of patience.

"Why have you come this day?" he sought to know.

"Once in a faraway country there were two wise men who sat before a fire all evening without speaking, and at the end when they parted one said to the other: 'It's been a grand night tonight,'" Bony said. "We sit here at this little fire and see many things in the jumping flame and the smoke which blows away to nothing. Do I ask you why you sit here in the sun all day? No, I see much in the flame of Gup-Gup's fire."

Gup-Gup said: "Give it bacco, Boss."

"What," softly exclaimed Bony, languidly spurting smoke at the Chief. "Run out of bacco already? I can't believe it. Your lubras will still have plenty. How come you are short?"

"Bacco ration not come," growled Poppa. "Things are crook."

"That bad, eh! Well, you could both go to gaol. They hand out plenty tobacco in gaol. Not a bad place to be in. Bit lonely at night, though. No lubras to keep an old body warm, Gup-Gup. Bit of hard work for you, Poppa. But, as I said, plenty of bacco."

"Cunnin' feller, eh?" Poppa almost shouted.

"Tisn't hard to be cunnin' with you two dopes," Bony said, pleasantly.

"Cunnin' feller," Poppa repeated, and Bony proceeded.

"Tellin' yarns like the one about Lawrence and Wandin running away to Eddy's Well. Saying they were to be married and Captain telling about them beating the gun. And Wandin married to Mitti all the time, and Mitti going crook in front of Missus 'cos he thought she'd marry Wandin to Lawrence." Bony's voice rose a couple of octaves. "What's the matter with you? Go on, speak up. What's wrong with you pair of cackling lubras? How come you get initiated as young men?"

"Cunnin' feller," Poppa said again, and significantly Bony tapped his forehead.

"Wonky! No doubt about being wonky, both of you. You got it good. Good camp. Plenty of water. Plenty tucker. Plenty bacco. No work. All your secret places to visit. Your young men and lubras to initiate, and then have them keeping your wood piles high. And you're that wonky you go and put over a tale of Wandin and Lawrence running off."

Poppa's face was working hard on the rage eating him. The moth-eaten white beard and scant hair of his chief shook slightly in the sunlight, and the skinny claws of hands gently pushed the ends of the fire-sticks together. His face remained empty, calm as that of the ivory Buddha. Suddenly the dynamic Poppa was on his feet and he was shouting down at Bony in his native language, eyes flashing redly like the fire in black opals, lips drawn back to reveal the teeth already beginning to decay.

Bony continued passively to smoke his cigarette. Gup-Gup spoke, sharply, without looking up, and the tirade ebbed like a high wave, to leave the man's hissing breath as the sand being washed by retreating water.

Poppa squatted on his heels, and Gup-Gup put a hand inside the mouth of the dilly bag of kangaroo skin suspended from his neck and produced a stick of tobacco and an old bone-handle clasp knife. Having nicked a chew from the stick, he replaced it and the knife, and solemnly stared at his fire as his prominent jaw worked. Following a spell of ten minutes of brooding silence, Bony continued with his prodding.

"Then you go to kid Captain to tell the Boss it was Lawrence out at Eddy's, and that he got sort of trapped by me and Young Col. You beat me. I don't get it. A little boy carried by his mother wouldn't have told that silly yarn to the Boss. And then sending Lawrence and Wandin with Captain to the Boss, saying they were to be married black-feller fashion some time. And walking away out from the Boss and leaving all their tracks in the compound for me to see the next morning and know it wasn't Lawrence out at Eddy's but a feller called Mitti. You askin' to go to gaol? Go on, say something."

They pondered this request for five long minutes, slowly chewing, reminding Bony of Mister Lamb who appeared much more intelligent than either at the moment. Not that he underestimated them, for there is nothing more spontaneous in the aborigine than donning the mask of stupidity. Then came the break, proving that Bony's guess was right. Gup-Gup looked up and met his eyes.

"Like you said, it was Mitti out at Eddy's," he admitted, and Poppa became uneasy. "He's the wonky feller, like you say we're wonky. Never no good. Never work for the Boss. He thinks he's a wild feller sometimes. Sometimes he go bush for long time with no pants on, no nothing on, not even the pubic tassel. Not even throwing spear or woomera.

"All right. Then Young Col and you see black-feller with nothing on at Eddy's. You see black-feller getting away quick into the grass. No pubic tassel, no spear, no woomera, no nothing. Mitti say he's wild black, but you know wild black don't get around with nothing. Boss he go crook when Young Col tell him about Mitti supposin' to be wild feller. Boss go dead crook for station black running about naked. Says he won't have feller with no pants on. Only me, long as I stop in camp. Come night and Mitti still running around, so Captain gotta do something, and they have Lawrence and Wandin running around to put Boss off the track. Okay! Boss say black-feller running around with young lubra all right by him . . . out at Eddy's."

"This Captain feller," Bony prodded. "Pannikin Boss at homestead. Another wonky black-feller camping at the homestead by himself, looks like. He pannikin boss over you?"

"Captain feller's the son of my son," replied Gup-Gup,

his old eyes swiftly bright. "My son killed by the wild blacks. Captain be Chief some time."

Now Poppa spoke.

"Captain pretty near white-feller-black-feller. We have trouble, Captain fixes it. Now we have trouble, Captain fixes it. Now we have trouble about Mitti running around naked, and Boss says nothing doing like that, and Captain fix more trouble."

"Captain didn't. You all made a muck of it," countered Bony, happy at luring these two from stubborn silence, yet unhopeful of extracting anything of value. "Now you have to marry Mitti's lubra to Lawrence, and break all the taboos and have the young men and lubras laughing like hell at you."

"Captain fix that too," proudly claimed Gup-Gup. "Mitti went bush with his lubra. Be away on walkabout long time. No more trouble."

Bony waited for both men to look directly at him, then asked: "Did Mitti and Wandin go walkabout on Station horse, Star?"

The shutters fell. Gup-Gup tended to his fire-sticks.

"Boss and fellers out looking for Star. Star got out from horse paddock."

"Then you be happy if they find Star. If they don't track Star, then Boss will say Mitti took him. Then he'll have Constable Howard looking for Mitti and put Mitti in gaol for pinching a horse. Trouble! Captain's going to have a lot of trouble over that horse if Boss don't track him up quick. Think Captain'll fix trouble like that?"

"Captain fix it, all right," snapped Poppa.

"Let's hope so. What with a white-feller found dead in the Crater, and you putting up the yarn about Lawrence and Wandin, and the Boss roaring about one of his horses missing, Captain is going to have a lot of work to do. Missus was telling me if the Boss can't find Star he's going to have you all pushed out of here over to near the Aborigines' Penal Settlement. And you two, of course, inside the Settlement Gaol. Can't go on."

Bony snatched up a blazing fire-stick, saying: "This one dead feller in Crater." He snatched another stick: "This one trouble over Mitti and Wandin and Lawrence." The third stick he plucked from under Gup-Gup's nose: "And this one the missing horse, if he can't be tracked. One, two, three, all together, make Constable Howard say you give him a belly full, you all head for the Settlement." Placing the sticks as the Chief had arranged them, and numbering each when so doing, Bony clinched with: "One no matter. Two no matter. Three no matter. But one, two, three, together like that, pretty crook for you all."

It was then he received slight reward, for Gup-Gup was too anxious to deny the Crater affair by saying: "Why you say and say for black-feller trouble in Crater? Us blackfellers been here long time, and no white-feller trouble put on us. You say we live good at Deep Creek homestead like we didn't know it. What for we have white-feller trouble for nothing? You say we wonky fellers. You wonky feller all right. Crater feller not black-feller trouble." Gup-Gup regarded Bony with keen eyes although his voice was mild. He added: "You big-feller policeman, you say, eh?"

What motive did these people have for murdering a white man? The only motive, did they actually kill the fellow which he was reluctant to believe, would be on moral grounds. Certainly not for gain. They were too far advanced from their original isolation, before the coming of the alien race, to kill merely for the thrill of it, too soundly established on the white man's threshold, and thus they would react with violence only to crimes against them such as robbing their Treasure House or stealing a lubra. And even the latter crime would give men like Gup-Gup cause for hard thinking. Sitting there, eternally poking his fire-sticks, looking like a gargoyle, an unwashed aborigine, he yet possessed an intelligence probably above that of many itinerent whites. The answer had to be loyalty to some one or thing.

Bony made another effort by putting down some of his cards.

"You fellers say the Crater man not your black-feller trouble," he said, speaking slowly. "Now you tell me, eh? What for you have tracker look-see what I did at the Crater, what for tracker went there before sunup after I went there? What for you send lubra tracking me up the Creek same morning? What for you send black-feller standing outside my room at homestead? I say you don't like me prospecting the Crater, you don't like for me to find out who killed the Crater feller, who put him in the Crater. You tell me all these things, eh?"

"Cunnin' feller," Poppa said, softly.

Nothing further was said. The fine points of the white man's law could not be appreciated, such as being accessories after the fact, or even before the fact. The silence of an unbridgeable gulf descended upon them like a fog, barring him out and barring those two into their own limitless prison beyond the gulf. He smoked another cigarette before abruptly leaving them.

Instead of returning to the homestead he walked out into the desert and to a low range of sand dunes, and on a ridge he sat facing to the east and the south. He was feeling depressed, not by failure or from frustration, but by a sharp sense of his own limitations and inability to cross the gulf separating these people from himself. It wasn't the first occasion in his career when confronted by this gulf he felt resentment that his mother had given him only half of himself, her own race, the other half bequeathed by his father and so placing upon him a schism to be likened to hobbles fastened to his feet.

The sun was low over the mountains, and the dunes cast their ragged shadows away to the east, and far beyond them was his own shadow like a pointer indicating Lucifer's Couch. Well, if Gup-Gup and Company told the truth when denying killing the man in that Crater, then they must be acting loyally towards those who did. It must have been a white killing, and the people for whom they acted in loyalty must be among those at the homestead. To whom? All or only one man at the homestead. If only one, to which of them would they be loyal?

Behind him sounded the hooves of galloping horses, and turning he saw Young Col and an aborigine riding homeward. Young Col waved and shouted: "Who wouldn't be Inspector Bonaparte?"

16

BONY CHAMPIONS
THE ABORIGINES

At dinner that evening Bony heard of the failure by the musterers to locate the absent horse. Brentner and each white stockman had taken a black stockman with them, and thus in pairs had ridden all day in effort to cut the animal's tracks. All had to report no result, and each had hoped to find a lucky pair back before their own arrival at the yards. They were mystified and angry when they met at table, and Brentner wisely left the subject to his two assistants.

"I reckon Inspector Bonaparte pinched that moke," Young Col said, speculatively regarding Bony. "He's away on walkabout, and Star is missing. It follows, you know. Deductive reasoning. When are you going to bring him back, Bony?"

"Matter of fact he went lame and I left him at Beaudesert," Bony replied. "It's why I didn't get home until late this morning."

"And us working all day and wearing out the seats of our pants looking for him," avowed Old Ted, winking at Tessa. "Nice how-d'you do wasting the Company's money in wages. You must have grown wings to the blighter and flew him to Beaudesert. Got lame in one of his wings, I suppose."

"Ran out of petrol more likely," submitted Young Col,

watching Old Ted. "Anyway, now that the Star mystery is solved, Mr. Brentner, who are you letting go to Hall's for the conference tomorrow? Me, I hope."

"I haven't decided yet. I haven't even decided if I'll go," replied Brentner, a trifle shortly. "I'm not liking this Star business. Horses don't vanish on me and get away with it. What with our own blacks going wild and the wild blacks wild all the time, the country is going to pieces. I had Captain with me and he acted like he had the stomach ache all day. What did you fellers do? Go to sleep under a shady tree until it was time to come home? Horses can't walk around without leaving tracks. One pair of us must have crossed 'em, with our eyes shut."

The three men fell into moody silence. Rose Brentner glanced at everyone by turn. The children concentrated on the meal, and the young aboriginal girl watched Brentner with what Bony thought was admiration. Presently Bony said: "Saying that you thought Captain must have had a tummy ache, gives me an idea about the missing horse. I see that the horse paddock contains a fair number of low trees and a good deal of desert scrub. Supposing Star had a tummy ache and was lying down separated from the other horses. He might still be lying down: by now he might be feeding with the other horses. If you like, I'll ride over that paddock tomorrow. I once knew a horse that would deliberately lie down when he saw anyone coming for him, and another horse I knew used to hide behind a tree."

"There you are," remarked Old Ted to everyone. "Case terminated. The horse isn't outside the paddock, so he must still be inside. Quate simple, Watson. Quate. Next case, please."

"You aren't an old enough Pommy yet to ape 'em," chided Young Col. "Of course, Ted isn't a real Pommy. He was only born in England, but he likes us to think he was left on the steps of Buckingham Palace and was reared by Royalty. Puts on the dog now and then."

Brentner smiled sourly, and said to Bony: "I've got that information you wanted. If you care to come to the office we could take our coffee there."

"Ha! I've been hoping that would come through," Bony said casually, and followed the cattleman from the room. In the office, Brentner invited him to occupy an easy chair, and himself crossed to the window which he closed.

Neither man seemed anxious to begin, Bony engaging his fingers with his eternal cigarettes, and the big man standing at his desk and slicing shavings from his tobacco plug. It was Brentner who opened after lighting his pipe and taking the opposite chair. He spoke roughly, as though addressing a stockman.

"Well, what d'you know about that horse?"

"A little, and much. We are surrounded by a conspiracy of silence concerning the horse as well as concerning the murder of the man in the Crater. You won't like it, but I decided it would be sound strategy for you and your men to spend an entire day looking for the horse."

Brentner's brows rose and then sank to create a savage scowl.

"I'd like to hear more," he said.

"First let me recall a conversation we had the other evening. I expressed the opinion that your aborigines probably know who killed the man and who put his body in the Crater, and were not necessarily directly involved. I am still hoping that that opinion will be supported by the facts which ultimately will be disclosed concerning this murder. If that should be the outcome of my investigations I shall do all I can to side-step pinning on them the charge of being accessories after the fact. You already have my reasons for that, and would doubtless be in full

agreement. Now, can you assure me of continued co-
operation?"

"Damn it, I don't know if I'm coming or going. If you
want me to acknowledge you as the boss in the affair, all
right."

"I am, indeed, the boss in this affair," Bony went on.
"I needn't repeat a single circumstance relative to the body
and the place where it was found. A man was murdered
with a blunt instrument as the police doctors name the
application to the head of a heavy object. Certainly a job
for the Police anywhere in the world. It is the motive not
the deed itself which is of paramount interest to my supe-
riors, and the motive, I am convinced, is concealed in the
minds of your aborigines, or the minds of a neighbouring
tribe. And there is no need to stress to you the difficulties
hedging aboriginal psychology. I will therefore . . . I
hear . . ."

The door was opened a moment later, and Rose Brentner brought in the coffee tray.

"I wanted to be in this exchange of confidences," she
told them, and Bony took the tray from her and placed it
on a side table.

"I've been anticipating that you would," he told her,
smilingly. Crossing to the door, he turned to add: "We've
been talking about politics and the visit of the Minister
to these parts." Closing the door, he stood with the handle
remaining in his hand, they looking at him in amazement.
Continuing in raised voice, he said: "You should have an
enjoyable experience at the conference tomorrow, hearing
all the vague but glowing promises of the future of this
great North of Australia."

Abruptly opening the door he stepped out into the passage, glanced both ways, re-entered and said calmly: "I've
been telling your husband I had to let him and his men

look all day for a horse, which isn't, as a counter move against those opposed to my investigation."

Neither commented, the man still dour and the woman still astonished. Without intention of being provocative, Bony resumed his chair and rested his chin on his tented hands, regarding them almost absently before saying: "The aborigine discovered by Young Col and me at Eddy's Well was one called Mitti, the husband of Wandin. You couldn't find the horse, Mr. Brentner, because the horse is dead."

The blood reddened Brentner's face, but his voice was controlled.

"Where did you find it?"

"Mitti rode the horse hard to arrive at the Well before we did. It collapsed under him. Wait a moment. The aborigines are not to know what we know, because it will be through their actions we shall learn the motive for the Crater crime, as well as the man, or men, who committed it. Can you continue to assure me you will both co-operate?"

"Certainly," instantly replied Rose Brentner. She regarded her husband with impatience at his hesitancy before nodding. "What's on your mind, Kurt? Of course, we must co-operate with Inspector Bonaparte. Don't you realise that if Mitti and Gup-Gup and Poppa and the others are implicated it could mean drawing Tessa and Captain into the affair?"

"Probably no if about it, Rose. I wasn't thinking of Tessa, but of Captain. He was rebellious today, and I don't forget it was Captain who managed that runaway lovers' act the other evening. What I've thought and often said is that an abo, and white men, too, for that matter, can get above themselves with a bit of learning. We'll co-operate, Bony."

"I didn't doubt you would," said the pleased Bony.

"Now do so this way for a beginning. Undertake the trip to Hall's Creek as you planned. You will be taking the children with you, I think it was understood. And take Old Ted too. You might leave Young Col, for he told me he can operate the transceiver. Agreed?"

"Yes. But Old Ted didn't say he wanted to go."

"I want him to go. You invent the reason why he should. If he stays there could be trouble again between him and Captain."

"So you heard about that? I suspected it but didn't know for sure."

"What trouble?" asked Rose.

"Woman trouble," her husband said. "Ted put up the tale some time back that his horse threw him and he was dragged by the stirrup and got his face damaged. I didn't believe it, and I didn't want to make a fuss if one of the abos had fought him over advances to a lubra. I've found it best to let the abos look after their own, which they can do all right."

"Then you had better get rid of him. We don't want that sort of thing going on."

"We had an agreement, Rose," Brentner reminded his wife, his eyes hard. "You run the homestead; I run the men and the cattle. We can leave approaches to the lubras by any white man to Captain. Captain can fight like a threshing machine. I'm not sacking Ted Arlie. He's a good cattleman, and will become even better. Besides white men are hard to get up here, that is, the kind of men we want to live with."

"Very well." Rose turned to apologise to Bony for the disagreement. "We'll find reasons for taking Ted with us. There'll be room enough. You will be staying?"

"Yes. I shall have Young Col to man-handle the radio if necessary. I could manage, but might not be here. I shall be hoping that, with the Top Brass at Hall's Creek, Gup-

Gup and Company will make a wrong move or two. You might, Mr. Brentner, instruct Captain to have a horse available should I need it, and you could leave orders with Col which would keep him handy to the homestead. Agreed?"

"Can do," assented Brentner. "Tell us where you found the horse. Tell us a bit more of what's been happening. We went out as far as Eddy's Well. Mustered through the grass too. You say the horse foundered, but we didn't see the crows at work on the carcase."

"I'll tell you this much, because I do want you to be clear in mind that your aborigines are mixed up in this murder in some way. I believe they are so acting under duress, fear of some thing or persons stronger than themselves. Or under a sense of loyalty to some person or persons who was actually responsible for the murder. I can think of no probable motive for them to be concerned in killing that white man. Twice Gup-Gup admitted to me that the consequences of such a crime would be disastrous for his people, and therefore it is extremely unlikely that he or his Medicine Man engineered it. You know how close knit these particular people are and the unlikelihood of any one of them acting independently.

"I believe they are under duress, or activated by loyalty, because from the moment I arrived I have been expertly tailed and no hostile act has been done to me. Mitti rode the horse to observe what I did at or near Eddy's Well. How he sneaked the horse away is no matter. He had to ride hard to get there first. When a mile from the Well in the grass the horse dropped dead, throwing Mitti forward to gash his forehead against a root. Subsequently, I watched the horse being cut up and the portions carried away. The cattle in vicinity were driven on to the pad where the dead horse had been in order to obliterate its tracks, and I've no doubt that its tracks nearer home were also erased."

"Who cut it up? My blacks?" Brentner demanded to know.

"Not now! No more, please. I have confided in you, which is rare for me to do. You may trust me to keep always in mind the well being of your aborigines. For them all over Australia I have deep sympathy, and provided they are not directly implicated in this murder, their tribal homogeneity shall be guarded by me. Leave for the conference tomorrow in the knowledge that all will continue here normally."

Brentner stood to say: "All right, Bony. As you say. You're a strange man, and I've never met your like. Damn it, I need a drink."

He unlocked a cupboard and produced a bottle of whisky, and his wife went out for glasses. Bony chuckled, and said: "I'd like your permission to use this office while you're away. I shall not mind if you take the cupboard key with you."

17

THE ANXIOUS LOVER

Bony left the Brentners to collect writing materials and withdraw to the day-house. There he smoked and pondered on what he would write to Mrs. Leroy's sister to obtain through her certain information by radio to be understood by no one else. Here it was cool and quiet save for distant music coming from a radio in the men's quarters.

The letter written and sealed, his mind returned to the Brentners and the recent conversation with them. There continued a small niggling doubt of the man but none of the woman. She was the stronger character, her husband occasionally explosively dominant but always surrendering. He would understand the aborigines far more deeply than would his wife, and there could be a far closer alliance between him and Captain than appeared. Having been all his life in this quarter of Australia he would be able to think as the aborigine, when for his wife they would still be remote. Bony could not side-step the possibility that Brentner knew something of the unknown white man found on Lucifer's Couch.

His task of uncovering the killer was made more difficult by lack of certain knowledge when being assigned. The superior person who asked if he could grasp this limited assignment did not inform who the man was and of his previous activities. He wanted only to know how the man came into this district without being reported, and what he had been doing. On being pressed he had replied that it was the work of the police to nail the killer, for in this his department wasn't interested.

Opposed to Bony was a wall, a wall of shuttered minds, a wall built to bar back the truth. This wall enclosed the Deep Creek homestead and aboriginal camp. The wall could, however, enclose Beaudesert homestead and camp, even other homesteads and camps farther distant. Brentner had agreed to co-operate with his efforts to topple the wall, but had contributed nothing of significance to its toppling. Bony felt that the cattleman knew of the wall and wished it maintained: possibly as many people having witnessed a crime hurry away to avoid being concerned with it.

Recent events had produced reluctance in Brentner to attend the conference at Hall's Creek with the touring Minister, but his wife had supported Bony as agreed, and should Brentner's reluctance to leave the homestead spring from other than the loss of the horse and the circumstances around it, then he must be confident that Bony would not topple the wall.

Now, when sitting at the table in the day-house, Bony was feeling satisfaction that the Brentners and one of their white stockmen, Old Ted, would be off the scene for a day or two during which he could continue to prod Gup-Gup and Captain, dig a little into Tessa, and converse at length with Jim Scolloti. With the Brentners absent, the wall might be less strongly based. In other words: divide and conquer.

It was then that Old Ted joined him, saying: "Could see you sitting here dreaming O My Love of Thee. I'd like a word with you. Okee?"

"Yes, why not?"

The red-bearded man was troubled. He sat at the table beside Bony and rolled a cigarette. He looked at the superscription on the envelope of Bony's letter, almost without intent, and having lit the cigarette he said: "The Boss just told me I'm to go with them to Hall's in the morning. I told him I wasn't keen and that Col wanted to go. He said he had work for Col and that I go for experience and what not. You are not going?"

"I'm a police officer, not a cattleman."

"That's so." Old Ted sighed when emitting smoke. "Better talk softly. Someone could be outside with the ear against the grass. I could see you through it. What's in my mind is this. You've certainly stirred these people here into running around. D'you know you are being tracked?"

"Explain."

"The other morning you came from a walk up along the Creek. I saw Captain speak to one of the lubras, and she went up the Creek back-tracking you. Then that yarn about Lawrence and Wandin going bush out at Eddy's Well was all eye-wash too. I saw Lawrence that same afternoon. I was up on the tank stand testing the water gauge, and I could see him in the camp."

"You did! Why then didn't you say so when Captain brought him and the lubra in here?"

"Because I'm giving Captain enough rope to hang himself."

Bony made no comment, and Old Ted delayed speaking again for a full minute.

"You knew that the next morning when you were looking at the tracks they left in the compound, comparing Lawrence's tracks with those made by the chap at Eddy's Well. I might be able to give you a lead. I don't know, but I might be in the position to, because I've been tracked quite a lot. They don't track me without a reason and they don't track you without one. And Captain's behind all the tracking."

"You don't like him?"

"No, I certainly don't," Old Ted unhesitantly admitted. "The Boss thinks the sun shines on him. In fact, if he thought Col and I would take it he'd make Captain a sub-manager over us. I don't like him for many things."

Ted fell into moody silence until Bony prompted: "You are not alone in that. Young Col dislikes Captain too."

"Now look! I'm in a jam, having to go to Hall's with the Boss. I'll have to tell you something not to my credit. Captain and I got into holts a few weeks back, and he licked me. I'm pretty good, but he floored me and I didn't like that. Bad enough to be licked by a white man. That fight was the climax of a lot of bad blood, and I'm telling you it's over Tessa. I've been sunk on Tessa for several years, and I'd marry her tomorrow or any time. She's a fine lass, you must know."

Following another moody silence, Bony offered encouragement.

"Tell me more. From when it began."

"Oh, it began before the murder. It came to a kind of head when we got home from the muster in April and I heard about the tribe going bush and Captain and Tessa with 'em. And then Tessa coming back with Captain and half her clothes torn off. I made her tell me what happened."

"What did happen?"

"Tessa told me that after running off with the mob she remembered what she owed the Brentners. She left the mob and was on her way home when Captain waylaid her and tried to take her. She had to fight him off. I nearly got stuck into Captain that time. A couple of days after that, we all went to the Crater to give the place a final look-see for tracks which didn't add up. It was then I became conscious of being trailed. Told Young Col and he checked and so found we were both being trailed. Why? I could understand being trailed here at the homestead on Tessa's account, but not Young Col. Seemed to be only one reason, which was to check on what we might discover about the crime."

"Can you remember where you were when becoming conscious of being trailed?" Bony asked, and Old Ted regarded him doubtfully. "Was it when you were inside the Crater and under the dip in the wall?"

"Yes, it was. How the hell did you know that? I remember Col and me standing there, and I was telling Col that would be the easiest place to lug a dead man over when there was Captain standing just behind us. Is that place important?"

"Hardly. What happened then? What did Captain say to it; I mean your theory?"

"Nothing. He saw we cottoned to him and went on tracking ahead, and soon afterward another buck seemed to hang behind us. We didn't discuss the place, or theory as you express it, and forgot about it."

"Could not Captain have been behind you at that moment by chance?"

"I'll tell you why not. When Col and I agreed that another buck had taken Captain's place, I noticed that the Boss had a tail and so did Mr. Leroy. Howard had one of his own trackers with him all the time."

"Why a tail to each white man?" pressed Bony. "It was days after Howard and his trackers were first on the job."

"But Captain was with them every day," Ted countered. "No, I don't know why, but it does prove something. That something is Captain's over-plus interest in what might be learned about the crime."

"It could be. What else?"

"Only that every morning since that day I am tracked about the homestead. To find out if I visited Tessa, perhaps, during the night. I don't rightly know. I do know I am tracked every morning. More than once I've left my quarters after midnight and taken a stroll right round the outside of the compound fence, turned from the fence for a little distance and returned to it at a place I'd remember. Next morning I've watched one of the lubras following exactly my trail. I know the reason for it, but I'm damned if I know the reason for tracking us white men in the Crater."

"H'm! Interesting, Ted. Most," Bony conceded.

"Thought it might be." Old Ted looked appealingly. "There's the jam I mentioned. You'll be staying here. Would you do me a favor?" Bony nodded. "Would you keep an eye on Tessa for me?"

"I shall be doing that in any case. Do you mind telling me what Tessa's reactions are to, let us say, your advances?"

"Yes. I told her I loved her. I told her I wanted to marry her. She said she'd never marry a white man because Mrs. Brentner wouldn't stand for it. Then she grabbed my whiskers, pulled my head down, and kissed me and ran off."

The sentimental Bony smothered a sigh. The large weather-veneered hands on the table clenched and unclenched. Advice he knew would be resented, and, anyway, what advice could he offer? Time would be the only healer, but before Time could do its work there might well be another killing at Deep Creek. He said: "Leave Captain to me. And don't worry about Tessa. My judgment is that she can look after herself. She's older than we know. Now go to Hall's Creek in good heart."

They stood to leave. Old Ted essayed a grin.

"There's something else you might make head or tail of," he said and Bony sat again. "I was riding home along the motor track from Paradise Rocks and came across two straight poles. Funny place to leave them. When I was out that way again they weren't there. Now what would any-

one want with poles out in the desert? Wouldn't be to
pitch a tent, and anyway half a dozen poles would be
needed for that."

"How long were these poles? How big, or thick?"

"Oh, I'd say they'd be seven to eight feet long. Fresh
cut saplings. Looked to be a little thicker than my wrists.
Fairly straight."

Bony opened the writing pad and rapidly sketched the
position of the homestead with the Crater, and the Crater
with the Creek.

"Put in the track from the homestead to Paradise Rocks
and then mark where the poles were seen. And the date."
He watched the dotted line being drawn from the homestead to the south-east, passing southward of the Crater.
He waited whilst Old Ted paused to consider before placing a small cross. "Good! Now the date."

"Let me think! It was the day I came back from de-
livering cattle to Beaudesert. I know. It was April 24. We
all had a spell day on the twenty-fifth, being Anzac Day.
Think it's important?"

"Could be," replied Bony. "When was it you noticed the
poles had disappeared?"

"Couple of weeks later. I was riding that way to look-
see what cattle were south from the Crater." Old Ted was
now tensed, and with some eagerness he waited for
Bony's next question. He was passed the rough sketch and
requested to be as accurate as he could with the cross,
alter its position if necessary. "Where I've put it would
be right," he said, and Bony was satisfied.

"You said you saw the poles that day you returned from
Beaudesert, Ted. You would pass north of the Crater, not
south."

"That's true enough. I sent the blacks home via the
Creek, and I rode out five miles south of the Crater to

check if cattle were sticking to a strip of fairly good feed. Boss asked me to."

"An oddity. I like them, Ted. Quite often one is significant. You are being helpful. Can you remember if the poles had been cut with a saw or an axe?"

"Yes, I can. They were sawn at both ends. What was damned funny about them was that they were freshly cut, and yet there were no tracks of a car or a horse or a man anywhere near."

"And you said nothing of it to anyone?"

"That's so," replied the bearded man. "I've been trying to work this thing out, but got nowhere."

"H'm! Tell me, have you ever seen anyone wearing as a charm a small ivory Buddha?"

Old Ted slowly shook his head, then said hopefully: "Saw a Buddha tattooed on a man's chest. Some time back."

"Tell me about it: where, when."

"I recall where. It was at Hall's. There was a party of Indonesian students touring through to Darwin. Stayed overnight at the pub. You know, usual washrooms off the yard. Feller was shaving next to me. The Buddha was tattooed light blue on his chest. You bring it to mind. About three inches by two."

Pretending disinterest, Bony asked for the approximate date.

"When! Let me think. June or July of 1959. Yes, June of that year. Any use to you?"

Speaking slowly, Bony said he didn't think so, and having gained Ted's promise to say nothing of any part of the conversation, they left for their rooms.

18

A SCOLDING FOR TESSA

A stranger might have thought the Brentners were leaving on a trip round the world. Outside the compound gate Young Col was servicing the large car and Old Ted was stowing suitcases in the boot. Inside the gate Jim Scolloti was controlling Mister Lamb by a trap about his neck and the two children were saying good-bye to both man and animal. About the out-buildings all the aborigines, including even Gup-Gup, had gathered to watch the departure. They were in cheerful mood as Brentner had instructed Young Col to issue the tobacco ration.

As the car moved off to take the Creek crossing the women and children waved, and from the horse-yards Captain shouted. Bony was left with Tessa and Young Col, when the cook stalked back to his kitchen, taking Mister Lamb with him to receive a shred of tobacco.

"Sorry you were not with them, Col?" Tessa asked, and Bony caught the mischievous gleam in her eyes. "Never mind. I'll look after you and Bony."

Young Col tossed his fair hair back from his eyes and pretended to reach for her with his grease-smeared hands, and there was on his face nothing of disappointment.

"You will be looking after us, my Tessa," he said. "I am the great big Boss of Deep Creek, so you keep that look out of your opalised eyes and don't waggle your bottom at us. Bony's an old married man, and I'm a confirmed woman hater. So you don't do anything. I'm off to manage the station. See you at ten o'clock smoko. Hooroo!"

For a moment or two Bony and the girl watched him proceeding to the store room, and then Bony said he'd like to see Tessa's book of legends. During the next hour they sat on the verandah, the girl sewing and Bony reading the neat handwriting in the book sold as a company minute book. When putting it down he was surprised by Tessa's literary ability.

"I think, Tessa, you will go a long, long way. You continue to astonish me," he told her.

"Thank you. It comes easily. Do you think any of them are false legends?"

"Yes. I doubt that two are genuine. They fail because in true aboriginal legends there is never prediction of the future: it is all of the past. So the one about the coming of the white men, and then the brown men, is obviously not a true legend. Where did you hear it?"

Tessa was looking at Bony with puzzled eyes. He could see she was trying to remember.

"I think it was in the camp," she said. "Some time ago. It wasn't long after I started to collect them into the book, and it's two years since I started. What's the other one you think isn't true?"

"The last one entered." Bony smiled, and his blue eyes were beaming with humour. "The one about the old lubra and the children who found legs of beef in the baobab tree. You see, I made that one up."

"You did! I thought that was good too." Tessa laughed with him. "I shall have to be careful. You're very deep, Inspector Bonaparte."

"It comes easily," he mocked her. "But, seriously, last night I jotted down several to relate which I'm sure are genuine. You must hear them before I leave at the conclusion of my investigation. Would you permit me to speak candidly about something else? You will remember that we agreed we shared a little secret, the powerful influence which kept us from returning to the Tribe. Remember? It was pride in accomplishment. You have so much reason for pride that I would like to point out what might well be disaster for you. May I?"

Her dark eyes were wide, luminous with intelligence, and yet he was aware he would have to choose his words else the shutters would fall. He thought she was seeking for deceit before saying: "All right."

"Now I'll begin by stating what I think to be true. For nine years, I think it is, you have been removed from your people and have lived in the sunshine of Rose Brentner's strong affection, and Kurt Brentner's strong protection. You are eighteen, and a woman. I can't be sure but I believe none of the young men at the camp has interested you, and that you have given much more thought to education than to boys of your own age. You have given more consideration to becoming a teacher because you want to be one, as well as because you know Rose wants you to be, than you have to marriage.

"I've been seeing you as Rose sees you, but there are others who don't see you as we do. I've found here a situation which could erupt into an explosion in which you also would be engulfed. There was that fight between Old Ted and Captain. There's Young Col worrying over Old Ted. Captain and Old Ted are two kegs of gunpowder, and you are the match which might blow them and yourself to bits. It was I who insisted on the Brentners taking Old Ted with them."

He had seen astonishment, alarm, resentment, flow and ebb in her eyes, and was hopeful when the shutters had not fallen as now she gazed at him with appeal. He said: "Far from blaming you, I feel sure you are not fully aware of the danger threatening because you have been so well protected that much younger girls at the camp know more than you of love. In this respect you have been placed to great disadvantage. I understand only too well the barriers by which you are surrounded, and this subject is no concern of mine excepting that we share the knowledge of the ever-present danger to the status we have achieved. May I go on?"

She was gazing beyond him to the creek trees when nodding assent. He thought the moment had arrived to whip lightly: "I suppose you don't know that after the fight Old Ted oiled and loaded his rifle, and that it was Young Col who turned him from going after Captain. Think what would have resulted from the death of Captain, how you would have been ruined. You see, girls all over the world and of all races waggle their behinds at men, and are seldom hurt. But you can't do that without courting your own destruction. As I stand physically between two races, you stand mentally between those two races. Tell me, do you love Old Ted?"

"I like him. I don't know about loving him," she admitted, still gazing at the distant trees. "He asked me twice to marry him. I don't think I could. Rose would never forgive me. I don't want to marry Captain, either." The tears filled her eyes when she turned them on Bony. "I don't want to marry anyone. I just want to go on as I am, not to be another lubra in a wurley under a tree. I—I waggled my bottom, as Col says, only in fun. I didn't mean anything else by it. You understand so much you must understand how confused I am sometimes. There's things I can't take to Rose Brentner."

"Because she would not understand. I know that, Tessa. No white woman could. Would you think about a spot of advice from grandpa?"

The answering smile was like a sand dune emerging from cloud shadow.

"Permit pride to take a firmer hold upon you. Always keep vividly in mind that you are Tessa. You don't belong to anyone. You are an aborigine woman but you don't belong to any aborigine man. You don't belong to anyone, not even to Rose Brentner to whom you owe so much. The only person who owns Tessa is Tessa. Get that clear in your mind and all the confusion will vanish. Want some more from grandpa?"

Her nodded assent betrayed eagerness.

"Well, then remember you can't help having loyalties which sometimes war with each other. You can't help being loyal to your own people as well as to the Brentners. The pity is that sometimes you cannot be loyal to both at the same time. For instance, the other evening you felt you had to be loyal to your people over the tale of Lawrence and Wandin, and then found yourself being conscious of disloyalty to the Brentners. Loyalties are a problem, and I know it. The only solution is to learn to be only Tessa, the Tessa who will decide for herself. And as for the men, you'll know when you fall in love with one, and then you must decide about marriage without reference to others."

Standing, Bony proffered the legend book, saying: "Meanwhile, I have to earn my salary and work in the office. I want to ask one question which you may answer or not. Did you tell Old Ted that, when returning that day of the last walkabout, Captain caught up with you and tried to seduce you?"

"Yes. I did. Captain didn't do anything like that. I told Old Ted because . . . I told him to pay him out for patting my behind. I've always been sorry about it. Thank you for speaking as you've done. I think I've grown up a little. I'll have to, won't I?"

Bony thought it a pity she should have to, and passed to the office where half an hour later Tessa found him browsing through the station work diaries and called him to morning tea. Young Col was already in the day-house, and he was welcomed with the usual flippancy.

"You must be exhausted, Bony, old feller-me-lad," Col surmised. "Tessa says you went to the office to work. Thought detectives never worked: just walked about and collared the criminals."

"We have to pass the time between collaring criminals. I've been looking through some of the early work diaries maintained by Leroy. Those early years must have been really rough. Two entries refer to a man named Wilcha. Ever heard of him?"

Col shook his head and Tessa replied for him.

"Chief of the wild blacks. Not now, though. He died. The present chief's name is Maundin."

"Good for you, Tessa," Col said, and took another of Scolloti's jam tarts.

"Ever seen Maundin?" Bony asked of Tessa, and she said she had.

"He visited Gup-Gup a few months ago. He didn't look so wild." The girl giggled. "He was wearing a long-tailed blue shirt and no trousers. Must have been a peace visit because he brought two lubras with him, and they didn't even wear a shirt. Horrible-looking things."

"The visit was, indeed, peaceful?"

"Yes, I think so. They didn't stay more than two days. When they went away, Gup-Gup and Poppa and Captain went with them somewhere."

"How long were Gup-Gup and Poppa and Captain away?" persevered Bony.

"Don't know about Gup-Gup and Poppa. I saw Captain back the next afternoon."

"So there is fraternisation at times between your tribe and the wild blacks," Bony said, apparently without much interest. "Someone told me of a place called Paradise

Rocks. I think it was you, Col. Is that the head camp of the wild blacks?"

Young Col thought not, and Tessa supported him, adding: "Went there once with Kurt. You come to it without warning. Go over a long rise and suddenly there are the rocks and the wattle trees among them. There's water bubbling up from the ground, and running away for a short distance and disappearing again into the ground. The blacks have guarded it against the cattle and buffaloes by rolling rocks all round. The trees were in blossom too."

The girl's eyes were shining. Her hands fluttered when describing Paradise Rocks and the bubbling water in the heart of the desert. She was wearing a white blouse and skirt and white shoes. A diamond-studded bar brooch caught the neck of the blouse from widening too deeply, and on the second finger of her left hand was a moonstone set in gold.

This was the picture of her Bony took back to the office, and there he asked silently what had Rose Brentner really achieved? The girl actually wore her clothes with the subtle distinction that Rose wore hers. Her voice was not unlike that of Rose Brentner, the enunciation clear and without accent.

Bony recalled that Tessa had appeared to emerge from the background of Deep Creek, to advance slowly but with progressive impact. And now after Rose had gone off Tessa was vivacious and belonged to Deep Creek homestead when Rose Brentner just failed to give that impression. Bony thought it probable that Rose did not know what she had done with this aborigine girl. She had omitted sex instruction, had relied upon the isolation of the homestead and her guardianship to prevent male advances, and thus Tessa's education was unbalanced, lopsided. The sooner Tessa was sent down to Teachers College, the better.

However, back to work. Tessa had named the chief of the wild aborigines, and had said he and his lubras had visited Gup-Gup, had stayed two days, and had departed in the company of his host and Poppa and Captain. It was sometime in March, the month prior to the murder of the white stranger. The two tribes were of the same nation, and they had been long in contact each with the other as proved by the treaty made between the wild blacks and Leroy and, after Leroy, Brentner. A visit, therefore, would not be unusual.

What might be significant was that when Maundin departed, the local chief and his medicine man, with Captain, went off with him and his lubras. Where to, and why? Especially with reference to Captain.

Bony had purposely refrained from questioning Tessa too closely. He wanted to avoid as far as possible testing her loyalty to her own people, feeling it to be unfair about a matter the elucidation of which might be obtained from other sources. For instance, Kurt Brentner's work diaries. The current diary was on the top of the desk.

Bony began at March 1. He came forward to March 31, and found no mention of Captain's absence. As Tessa might have mistaken the month, he ran over the notes for February, and then began with April 1. Ah! The girl had been mistaken. Under the date April 19 Kurt Brentner had written: "Captain reported Chief Maundin in the camp, and asked for tobacco. I let him have two pounds of plug to keep the wild bastard sweet."

Bony remembered he had asked Brentner had there occurred anything at all unusual during this period, and it would seem that the visit by Maundin was not thought to be unusual . . . save to note it in the work diary.

19

FUN AND PROGRESS

Bony read Brentner's work diaries in reverse order. The entries were succinct, often single words to continue a previous note, the total merely a guide to station activities rather than description. Eventually he came to an entry made the previous August which read: "Captain reported that yesterday two strange abos from the coast had visited the camp and left again before sundown. Captain had evidence on his face of a fight but refused to talk about it other than saying, I quote: 'No foreign scum is upsetting our people.'

"I visited the camp and found everything quiet. Useless to cross-question Captain when obstinate, and it's their business anyway."

Bony read over another year, and learned only about station and cattle and waterings, and associated subjects. He was pondering upon the entry concerning the visit by the two strange aborigines when Scolloti played the lunch tune on his triangle. After lunch he watched Tessa departing in the direction of the camp and he sought Young Col. It was then two o'clock.

"I want co-operation, Col. It will take me a little time to get the transceiver operating as, I see, the model is very modern. I want to get on the air to Howard."

"All right, I'll show you."

The set having warmed up, Young Col moved a switch

and a man's voice came in telling someone what to do with a child badly scalded.

"The Quack," Col said. "Better let him have his say."

"I want to contact Howard before Tessa returns from the camp. Tune the volume down a little, that Scolloti and Captain won't hear." Young Col frowned with perplexity. "Where is that doctor?"

"At Base. I can cut in when he's finished and before someone else takes over." The doctor eventually saying that would be all, Young Col went on the air. "Deep Creek calling Constable Howard. Come in Constable Howard. Deep Creek calling Hall's Police Station. Over."

A woman spoke. "Constable Howard out on duty. Can I take a message? That you, Young Col?"

"Too right it's me, Loveliest. Hold it." Then Col was reading his own version of the message Bony wrote on a pad. "Ask your Old Man if anything of an unusual nature occurred at coast ports round about present date one year ago, and report to Deep Creek at five tonight. That's all, and bless you, my child. Over."

"The last dance is tomorrow night. You're not my father. You're only a child yourself. I've got the message." The doctor spoke: "You children quit. Are you on the air, Kemsley Downs? Over."

Young Col shut down and turned to Bony, and was invited to sit on the verandah.

"I have a small commission for you to undertake as near as possible to five this evening," Bony said. "I want you to get that reply from Howard, talking as quietly as you can. I shall need to watch for possible snoopers. When you have heard from Howard, contact Mrs. Leroy. She will be waiting. Now I've asked her to answer several questions with either yes or no. She will say she has your wordagram and then say: One stroke ten, or one stroke five. Two stroke ten or two stroke five, as applicable to each question. Get it?" Col nodded. "I've asked several questions, so be prepared to record accurately Mrs. Leroy's replies. Clear!"

"As a bell." Young Col grinned. "Am I your Doctor Watson?"

"You are, my child. Meanwhile not a word, for the walls have ears. I shall see you at afternoon tea. For me, meanwhile, back to my sleuthing."

Bony found the cook enjoying his afternoon rest-spell, and on the way had paid Mister Lamb his toll of a cigarette. Scolloti was reading a ten-days-old sporting paper, and welcomed Bony with bright black eyes and a grin at the pet sheep who thrust his head in over the door step.

"Jim, I think I can diagnose Mister Lamb's recent bad form at Snooker," Bony said, sitting on the form flanking the kitchen table. "I believe he has a grass seed in his offside eye."

"Cripes! You could be right, Inspector: you could at that. Would account for him mis-cueing, sort of slewing the ball left or right of the pocket. Let's do him over before smoko. You any good with sheep? I'm not. I'm a cattleman."

"Good enough for the job."

"Yes, that what's wrong with him. I never thought of a crook eye. I'll get us the barber's scissors."

Waving the scissors like a sword, the happy cook strode to the doorway and yelled for Captain. The aborigine came, his face a shade anxious, but the smile flashed instantly into his dark eyes on hearing why he was wanted. Scolloti gave him a shred of tobacco, and with it Captain snared Mister Lamb, laid him on one side, and knelt over him. Scolloti held the sheep's head, and Bony went to work scissoring the wool from about the inflamed eye.

"Right! You fellers hold him steady. He has a seed, or rather the seed pod, fairly deep in under the bottom lid. I'll want tweezers, and a rag and water to bathe it."

"Tweezers in the saddler's room, Jim," Captain said. "Hold his head, Inspector. The patient's pretty powerful, and he's got a wicked temper."

Bony took over the head of the prostrate victim, and the cook went for the instruments. The aborigine chuckled, and Bony encountered the laughter-lit eyes.

"Young Rosie was telling me you were pocketted, Inspector. You'll know how powerful he is without me saying it. Trouble is you forget he's around, and when you hear him there's no chance of stepping sideways."

"I'll not forget he is around. Once pocketted is enough."

The cook returned with the tweezers and water in a bucket. Again he held Mister Lamb's head firmly to the ground and Bony removed the seed pod and bathed the eye. He was advised to take the bucket and himself to the kitchen, and then Scolloti hastened after him, leaving Captain to jump away and run for his horse-yard. Mister Lamb, however, staggered to his feet and hung his head as though horribly ashamed of being man-handled, looking so dejected that Bony went to him with a cigarette and he held it under his nose. Mister Lamb instantly forgot the indignity, and made no attempt to charge as Bony backed into the kitchen.

"You know, Jim, Captain's a strange man for a full-blood," he said, rolling a cigarette. "Speaks like a professor. Reads a lot. I understand he's even writing the history of his tribe."

"Got a mission, so he says, Inspector. Says he aims to be a buffer, his word, between the blacks and the whites. When I asked him how he nutted up the idea he said Mrs. Leroy put him onto it."

"Splendid!" exclaimed Bony and meant it. "Fine idea when one thinks about it. Pity such a mission isn't duplicated elsewhere. He wouldn't stand for interference with the blacks by any stranger, I suppose."

Scolloti pulled his ragged beard, and when speaking his dark eyes were sombre.

"That black is a smart lad. Bit too smart, in my opinion. Has to be put into his box sometimes. You know how they come. He made a chopping block of Old Ted not so long ago. What about I don't rightly know."

"Looks for fight?"

"Can't say he does exactly," replied the cook. "Got into holts with a couple of abos some time back. Seems he took 'em on both at once, and he was the chopping block that time. I heard the laundry lubras talking about it when they was having their smoko."

"How long ago was that?"

"How long!" Scolloti pondered while filling his pipe. "Let me think it out. Wasn't this dry. Musta been last year. You interested?"

"Not particularly," Bony replied, aware that here there are but two seasons: winter dry, and summer wet. "I've been under the impression that Captain would sooner laugh than scowl."

"They're all like that, but you cross 'em up and find out."

Scolloti glanced at his clock, and said that the afternoon "smoko was on deck." Bony left him to wash his hands and eventually drink tea and munch buttered scones with Tessa and Young Col in the day-house. He was relating details of the operation on Mister Lamb when Captain appeared in the entrance.

"Hullo, Captain! What's worrying you?" enquired Young Col.

"Well, after fixing Mister Lamb's sick eye, I was thinking that the Inspector might take on his shearing," replied the man with a mission. "I've always done it but I'm not that good at it. Time he was sheared, now winter's almost over. Got a lot of wool to carry about all day."

"The wool doesn't hinder his speed," Bony pointed out,

and Captain laughed. "After being shorn he'll orbit the homestead under a minute. All right, I'll shear him. Get things ready. I hope the shears are in good shape."

"I'll hone 'em right away, Inspector. Thanks."

Captain could be seen through the grass wall hurrying to the saddler's shop, and then appearing to squat in the sun and spit on the stone. Tessa said: "I'm glad you consented to do it, Bony. Captain's very rough. Nicks Mister Lamb and leaves ridges of wool all over him."

"I might not be much better," Bony doubted.

"Couldn't be worse," Young Col assured him. They saw a young aborigine come to talk to Captain, and then race away past the yards. "He's gone to tell the tribe. You'll be having an audience."

Soon thereafter the audience arrived to hover behind the out-buildings, take cover behind the date palms and native bean trees even though there was the compound fence between them and Mister Lamb lying down and chewing his cud inside the compound. On Captain coming to the kitchen with the shears and an arm loaded with bags, Bony with Tessa and Young Col went out to meet him. Mister Lamb lurched to his feet and bleated from growing suspicion.

"Looks like he'll have to be done over where he can be snaffled," said the excited Captain. "He's remembering the eye deal, and he knows what the bags are for. I won't have a chance. You grab him, Col."

"Me! No fear. You have a go at him, Bony."

"It's a young man's job of work," objected Bony laughingly, and Tessa said: "I'll grab him. Make me a cigarette."

As she advanced upon the enormous pet sheep, her slight figure by comparison became a small child courting a Shetland pony. Mister Lamb permitted her to approach just within half a dozen yards of him, when he jumped to land on stiffened legs, and then proceeded towards her in short thudding props. Tessa called to him, and courageously kept walking, holding the cigarette to see with the one healthy eye. It must have been the girl rather than the bribe who conquered him. She gave him half the cigarette, and teased him with the remainder until he was more docile, when she passed an arm under his neck, gripped a fore-leg and threw him.

The audience shouted its approval, and Captain with Scolloti hastened forward with the bags to fashion a "floor" on which to shear, and the shears to shear with. Bony was presented with the shears. Mister Lamb was inelegantly lifted onto the bags, and Bony took him over, placing him on his rump with his back pressed to the shearer's legs.

Now the audience came to the compound fence and Scolloti leaned back against the door frame of his kitchen and lit his pipe. Captain hovered about Bony, ready to leap for a safe place if the shearer lost his hold. The entire homestead was hushed to funeral silence.

Mister Lamb had become a lamb, indeed, offering no opposition, resigned to this second indignity of the day. Bony removed the belly wool, trimmed the legs, opened up the fleece down the right side, and then kneeling on a hind leg, and with the left hand gripping Mister Lamb by the jaw, proceeded to remove the fleece without breaking it. Ultimately, his right hand cramped by the work it was called on to perform, he heaved Mister Lamb off the fleece and again sat him on his rump. Mister Lamb was as white as snow and one third his original size. Again the audience shouted.

Tessa and Captain came with more bags, and it was Tessa who gleefully rolled the fleece and carefully pushed it into the bag Captain held open to take it.

"Why, you haven't cut him once," she cried and Bony expostulated.

"Cut him! Of course not." He glanced about at the spectators beyond the fence. He saw the cook still leaning against his kitchen door frame. The spectators now fell into silence, appearing tense, expectant, eager for the next act, the next act being what Mister Lamb would do when released.

"Righto, Tessa, take the wool and the bags and toss the lot on the far side of the fence. And get over it too," commanded Captain. He waited until the girl did as bidden, and to Bony said: "Better let me take him, Inspector. Once loose he'll perform like a champion."

Gladly Bony accepted this offer and joined Scolloti. Captain meanwhile had Mister Lamb pressed back hard to his legs. He gazed at the audience which was literally holding its breath. He looked round at the day-house, then at the kitchen, then at the verandah steps, and he was like a batsman taking note of the field. Then, with a violent push he sent Mister Lamb forward to his four feet, and himself raced for the protection of the day-house, this being the closest haven.

Bony thought it would have been more sensible to have carried Mister Lamb and neck-roped him to a tree until his blood pressure had subsided. This, obviously, was not according to protocol. Mister Lamb glimpsed the fleeing Captain. He spun about and was amazed by his lightness. He felt able to fly. He felt wonderful as he sped after Captain, a pure white arrow tipped with blazing yellow eyes, for even the sick one was now again in use.

It was Captain's intention to round the day-house and so on to the sanctuary of the kitchen, but Mister Lamb by short runs and short leaps on the stiffened legs gained so fast that the aborigine darted into what he thought was the safety of the interior, knowing that Mister Lamb, after repeated expulsion, dare not enter. Mister Lamb, however, was smelling victory, and was blind to edict. He went in after Captain.

The entranced spectators listened to the whoops and laughter issuing from the day-house. Their shouted responses were cut off when Captain appeared at top speed, to make for the kitchen door through which the cook vanished. A swift backward glance appeared to convince the aborigine he would not make it, for he darted to the right and slewed Mister Lamb for the three seconds necessary to haul himself up and into a bean tree.

20

THE TREMBLING
FINGER POINTS

The hero of the local sheep-ring, wearing only trousers and appearing in the branches of the tree like a crow with a wounded wing, listened to the shouting of the men and excited screaming of the women, and was proud of his limited victory. Mister Lamb, however, was a continuing problem. He backed away and shadow-sparred, made short runs on iron-stiff legs, thudded his cloven hooves upon the arena, bleated defiance. He was now the boss cocky, and knew it.

If the Australian aborigine lacks an attribute it isn't courage, but as other men he dislikes being made to look ridiculous. Captain could have dropped to the ground, but Mister Lamb would explode upon him before he could begin the sprint to the fence. He slid down the trunk for several feet, and Mister Lamb's golden eyes became sadistic orbs. He climbed again, and this time went higher to a comfortable perch, and there he bit a chew from his plug and gave back a little he was receiving from the onlookers.

Half an hour wore away, and the situation remained static. Captain chose a branch from which he could drop clear. He tossed his tobacco plug to land at Mister Lamb's feet, but Mister Lamb refused to be side-tracked.

Captain could visualise being hurled through the air

and hearing the yells of the audience. He could see himself listening to the laughter. He could hear in advance the mocking shrieks of Tessa and of all the other young lubras. He decided to maintain mortified patience and wear out Mister Lamb's anger.

Thirty minutes later he was shouting for someone to lassoo the beast. No one volunteered, and he called on individuals, beginning with Young Col who urged him to wait in the tree until he could bring his camera. Bony claimed he was still too old. Tessa giggled and mocked, saying that Rosie's Little Lamb wouldn't hurt a great big lion tamer like Captain. The onlookers squatted on the ground, and, making Captain's situation appear a permanent one, Mister Lamb also laid himself down and with saturnine mien vigorously chewed his cud.

An hour later Bony told Young Col to wait for the denouncement and not bother with the transceiver, and he was ready when Howard came on.

"Reference your inquiry, there was a spot of trouble at Wyndham twelve months ago last June. Three Asian crewmen deserted from a lugger and went bush. One was subsequently apprehended at Darwin several months later, and the other two were found in Derby. Over."

"Thanks, Howard. Both Derby and Darwin are a long way from Wyndham. Were they reported on this radio network?"

"The men at Derby were not. The one picked up in Darwin was reported from Adelaide River."

"Thanks again. Have the Brentners arrived yet?"

"Yes. They're at the Hotel. The Official Party have arrived too. In camp near the Hospital. Big get-together tomorrow. Everyone in the Kimberleys will be turning up, I'm told. By the way, tell Col Mason my wife likes being called Loveliest but I'm not warmly in favor. Over."

Howard heard Bony laughing softly. Then: "I thought

he was addressing your daughter, Howard. I'll give him your message. Now I am calling Mrs. Leroy for a message to Mister Colin Mason."

Mrs. Leroy's voice came clearly.

"Inspector Bonaparte! Oh, yes I promised Col a few clues for his wordagram. How are you liking Deep Creek?"

"Wonderful. Peace and rest, Mrs. Leroy. Young Col is busy, and I consented with pleasure to contact you. If you will give me the clues for the wordagram, I'll jot them down and then ask you to tell me of something."

Mrs. Leroy gave the clues, concluding with hoping they would be of use.

"I thought I'd take this opportunity of asking if there was unrest among your aborigines last winter," Bony said, and Mrs. Leroy replied to the effect that their only trouble had been late in August when the local tribe had gone on walkabout just when their young men were needed for stock work. Otherwise no serious trouble. Bony thanked her and shut down.

On returning to the arena he found Captain still treed, Mister Lamb still inviting him to descend, Tessa still sitting on her box, and the cook automatically appearing in the doorway and disappearing to make progress with his dinner. Bony sat in the day-room and reviewed the conversations he had had with Howard and Mrs. Leroy.

In June of the previous year three members of an Asian lugger crew had deserted at Wyndham. Two of these men had reached Derby on the west coast, and the third had reached Darwin after being reported by radio at Adelaide River. Late in August of this same year two strangers had visited the Deep Creek aborigines and had fought Captain. Brentner had recorded these strangers as aborigines, and dismissed them. Were they the two Asians ultimately arrested in Derby? Brentner had written that Captain had told him that no foreign scum was going to upset his people. Brentner had also written in the work diary that Captain refused further information and that it was his tribe's business, anyway.

"No foreign scum" seemed to be a pointer which might be of interest to the Source from which Bony had accepted his assignment. He wondered if the Source had deliberately retained this information or had been too blind to give it significance.

The Source wanted to know how the man on Lucifer's Couch passed through the Kimberleys without being reported, and should have been interested in two Asians travelling from Wyndham to Derby without having being reported. However, the deserting Asians might have sailed from Wyndham on a Derby-based lugger, and Captain might have referred to the strangers as foreigners had they belonged to a distant aboriginal tribe or nation.

There were the replies to the questions submitted to Mrs. Leroy by letter, and Bony glanced at his notes.

QUESTION ONE. Have you heard a legend about the Crater? No.

QUESTION TWO. Have you heard the legend that after the white man would come the brown man, and after the brown man, the land would return to the aborigines? No.

QUESTION THREE. Have you ever seen a small ivory Buddha possessed by any person? No.

QUESTION FOUR. Reference to question three: worn as a talisman by any person? No.

QUESTION FIVE. Has Captain visited towns other than Derby? If so, give first letter. B. O. P. (Broome, Onslow, Port Hedland.)

These three towns are south of Derby, and doubtless Captain accompanied the Salvation Army Padre on a southern tour, during the period he was at school in

Derby. It was now becoming clear that Captain could answer the final questions.

The sun was setting, and Jim Scolloti, who was casual in everything save his cooking, was reminded of the time. He said something to Tessa, and Tessa proceeded to stalk Mister Lamb. Mister Lamb continued to watch the treed Captain and failed to see or hear the girl approaching at his rear. When he became aware of her it was too late to do anything than gratefully accept the shred of tobacco abruptly thrust under his upper lip. Another Samson betrayed by a woman, meekly he was carried by the Philistine Captain to the fence, heaved over it and aimed at the fleeing aborigines.

During dinner, Bony asked Col if there was a carpenter's shop in addition to the saddler's shop.

"Next to the saddler's shop," replied Young Col. "You wanting to make something?"

"Equipped with tools, of course? Who has normal access to it?"

"Anyone told by the Boss to do a job there. Always kept locked, and the key on a hook in the office. Tools are expensive, you know."

"How long ago did anyone work in the shop?"

"How long!" Young Col concentrated, and Tessa looked as though wanting to help. "It would be before the first muster this year. End of summer. Too busy with the cattle during winter. And there was no special job came up."

"It isn't important," Bony said, toying with biscuits and cheese. "Actually, I've been trying to fit a clue into your wordagram." Turning to Tessa, he explained: "Young Col has been exercising his brain on a puzzle called a wordagram. I'll show you how to make one later on." Turning back to Col he said: "Let's try again, Col. Just who would be sent there to work?"

"Oh, well, the Boss might tell Old Ted or me, even Captain, to do something needful. Then the drill is to get the key from the office, and return it to the office immediately the job was done. After locking up, of course."

"All types of tools there, I suppose."

"Everything."

"I believe I'm getting warm, Col. What about old worn-out tools? Would they be passed out to the aborigines, or left lying about?"

"No fear. When we indent for new things like tools, the old stuff has to be sent to the Agent at Hall's."

"What about axes and axe handles. Have they to be sent to the Agent?"

"Not axes and tomahawks, only carpenter and saddler tools."

"I'm still warm," Bony declared with enthusiasm. "But there is still the last time anyone worked in the carpenter's shop."

"The work diary would give it. I'll go and look if you wish."

"Perhaps I can tell you, Bony," Tessa cut in. "I remember that Rosie's work box came unstuck. We couldn't make the lid fit properly. Captain came for the shop key, and Rosie asked him to fix the box. He brought the box back when he returned the key."

"Wonderful, my Tessa, but what was the date?" Young Col insisted, and Tessa giggled triumphantly. She made them wait till she said: "It was the day Rose gave me a lovely jewelled hair comb on my official birthday. April the twentieth. Does that give the word for the puzzle, Bony?"

"Yes, it does, Tessa. The word is saw. It will fit perfectly."

Bony skillfully switched to the subject of the dance to be held at Hall's Creek this coming night, and then to the return of the Deep Creek party the following day. When

Tessa left for the coffee, he complimented Young Col on supporting him in the discussion about the wordagram and promised to explain further on the morrow. Eventually, he visited the office to refresh his memory. In the work diary under the date April 20, he read: "Ted left with cattle for Beaudesert. Col left to check cattle about Eddy's Well. Went myself to Laffer's Point to repair mill pump. Got back late, and Captain reported he had escorted Maundin off the premises as far as Eddy's Well."

Recalling that Tessa had been wrong on a date, he checked backward and forward in the diary and could find no mention of Captain being sent to work in the carpenter's shop.

Young Col found him meditating when he came to switch on the radio for the expected contact by Kurt Brentner, and thus Bony heard the cattleman say they had decided to stay in town for another day to attend the dance.

This suited Bony as he wanted to investigate the matter of the sawn-cut poles before tackling Captain. After breakfast the next morning he set about this, seemingly wandering down the Creek without purpose. He visited Gup-Gup and talked with him and Poppa. He made a casual enquiry of Mitti and Wandin and was told they were still away on walkabout. He wandered about the camp, casually examining the primitive wurlies, and noting that the poles and sticks of the framework supporting the bark and discarded iron sheets had all been cut with an axe.

In the early afternoon he sauntered up the Creek, pausing repeatedly to gaze idly at the scene whilst believing himself under constant surveillance. He tossed stones into the reservoir, drove a flock of cockatoos from a tree by tossing a stick among them, and, where the water shallowed, crossed the Creek, for in the bend grew clumps of gum saplings.

Here he found two which had been cut down at the height of a man's waist. Without stopping, he observed the gum blobs which had oozed from the parent stem and also at the end of the bushy heads lying on the ground. These still retained their leaves, now dry and beginning to turn from grey to riven yellow.

From these saplings had been taken the poles seen by Old Ted near Lucifer's Couch. The cutting tool had been a saw. A saw had probably been used because the sound of an axe would have been heard at the homestead.

21

CAPTAIN BURSTS A SEAM

Bony had afternoon tea with Young Col and Tessa, and through the thin grass wall of the day-house, watched Captain cross to the kitchen for his smoko tea, and later watched him, wearing a blue gown and canvas slippers, leave his hut for the shower house. When, half an hour later, Bony entered his hut he was wearing only cloth trousers, and his newly shaven face was shining almost as much as his combed hair.

The place was orderly and clean. The blankets on the trestle bed were folded in army style. The window was open and set against it was a table on the far side at which Captain was seated reading a book. He stared when Bony drew forward a packing case and sat opposite him, Bony's back then being to the door.

"'The time has come the Walrus said' . . . and you may know the rest," Bony began pleasantly, and fell to making a cigarette. "I hope I'm not disturbing you, but there are questions you could help me with."

Captain smiled, a smile as open as his eyes.

"I'll do my best, Inspector," he said, and waited for Bony to apply a match to the cigarette.

"Do you agree with me when I say it's my belief that the stranger's body was deposited in the Crater because the Crater, being of recent origin, is the only place not associated through history, custom, legends, with your Tribe?"

"You are right when you say the Crater hasn't any association with my people, being of recent origin," replied Captain, opening a tin of tobacco and proceeding to make a cigarette. "But as it must have been a white killing I'm sure, too, that they wouldn't bother about whether or not it had any connection with them."

"Sound logic, Captain, if it had been purely a white killing. I find myself opposed to that theory. I'm convinced that were it not a purely black killing, then it was half and half, meaning that the blacks had a part. Had the murder been done by whites only, they wouldn't have bothered to carry the body to the Crater, because, as you have admitted, they would have no possible reason for doing so. They would have buried or burned the body. They wouldn't have bothered, even had they thought of it, to stage a death from thirst and exposure. The whites alone couldn't be held responsible."

The cigarette made, Captain raised his eyes and regarded Bony whilst he held a match to it. His eyes were now blank, his features minus any expression. Bony continued.

"There are, of course, other matters I'd like to discuss additionally to your own unusual behaviour. I refer you to having had me tracked on several occasions. I refer, too, to the rather crude little play you staged with Lawrence and Wandin, and I think I'm entitled to be resentful of your contempt of my own capabilities."

Captain closed his book and pushed it aside against the raised window. He gazed at the scene of Creek trees and homestead, and the desert falling away to the rim of the world on which lay Lucifer's Couch.

"You will agree, I'm sure, that Gup-Gup and people at Hall's Creek are much more authoritative on when the

meteor fell than the amateur geologists who visited the
Crater only a few years ago. Gup-Gup and Company supported by the absence of aborigine legends about the
place must be right. Agree?"

Captain nodded, and turned again to look beyond the
window.

"Then you must agree that genuine legends are based
much farther back in time than sixty years. I recall reading
in Tessa's book a legend having a political trend, the legend of the brown man following the white man, et cetera.
She thought it was a genuine legend, and yet Mrs. Leroy
never heard of it. Did you imagine, create, that legend?"

"What if I did? It's no crime to invent legends."

"It is a crime to create a legend for a purpose other
than entertainment, or at the expense of investigating anthropologists. Now did you or did you not invent that
particular legend?"

Captain again stared out the window, and when Bony
insisted on a reply, his voice was sharp.

"I asked you a question, Captain."

"Yes, I did, and what of it?"

Bony was abruptly confronted by blazing dark eyes.

"I'll accept your answer pro tem. I'm told you have
long had a laudable ambition, that you have adopted a
mission. You yourself have supported it. I am in complete
sympathy with it. I believe that the crime in the Crater is
the result of a grave threat to that which you and I are in
accord. If you will believe that we are in accord, if you
will trust me to work out a way whereby your Tribe may
be relieved of certain drastic results still to follow, then
for the salvation of your mission, assist me by being open
and truthful. What is the significance of the little Buddha
in the Tribe's Treasure House?"

The question brought Captain to his feet. He began to
shout.

"The Treasure House is Poppa's concern. I don't know what's in it. I'm not a medicine man. I'm not an Old Man."

"I was speaking of the ivory Buddha, giving that more importance than where I saw it," Bony said, voice hard. "It represents a culture completely foreign to that of the Australian aborigine. Now, sit down, and be rational." Captain sat, and took time to regain normal stoical composure.

"Gup-Gup says you were boned one time," he said. "You could be boned again for interfering with the Tribe's Treasure House."

"That would, indeed, be very bad for me, Captain. And for you, of course. You would have a great deal to do to explain what lay behind the story of the runaway lovers. You would have to provide the Boss with reasons why Mitti rode Star to death, and why Poppa and others cut up the carcase and tossed the remains into a prospector's mine shaft. And so much more to explain too."

The aborigine's round and creaseless face was again turned to the window. Bony could just see the frown which settled for a moment, and which was followed by a firming of the outline of the chin. Then he was being regarded by eyes having no expression, blank eyes having no depth in the iris.

"The trouble with you," Bony continued, "the trouble with you is that you're placed at the same disadvantages as is Tessa. She heard your story of the runaway lovers and, although she knew Wandin is Mitti's lubra, she backed you in default. She was torn by two opposing loyalties, to her people and to the Brentners. Doubtless you have heard the truth that no man can serve two masters, and those who try invariably end in disaster. You are torn by the division of loyalties, as is Tessa. Now, Captain, you have to decide which master you are going to serve.

"In fact I think you have already made the decision to

serve your own people. If so, you have my admiration because you're able to serve them ever so much better
than the white race, or the brown, or the yellow. The aborigine in me cries to you to serve your people wisely, and
say and do any and every thing to extricate them from
the mess they have fallen into on the death of the Crater
man."

"They had nothing to do with it, as I told you," Captain
avowed, eyes suddenly blazing, and the shutters lifted by
the compelling emotion to safeguard his own. "Leave
them out of it, Inspector. Leave them alone. Leave me
out of it too. The killing was nothing to do with them."

"Then tell me why you had me tracked?" The shutters
fell before the eyes, barring in the mind behind them, and
Bony felt pity for the man wriggling on a hook, this man
particularly whose partial assimilation with the white race
had failed to withstand an influence yet to be disclosed.

"Tell me why you accepted the opportunity given by
Brentner's absence on April 20 to obtain the key to the
carpenter's shop from Tessa for the purpose of borrowing
a saw, a saw with which to cut two poles, fearing an axe
would cause too much noise."

"So little Tessa told you that, eh!" Captain's hands were
tightening their fingers about each other.

"Not consciously. Tell me why you cut the poles?"

"To make something."

"The frame of a stretcher to carry the body to the Crater. That required two men. The two men had wrapped
hessian bags about their feet to prevent tracks. They took
the body over the Crater wall at its lowest point. They
could not permit the body to remain on any part of the
Tribal Ground, every yard of which is hallowed by the
centuries." Bony's voice rose a fraction, and the words
were like a whip flaying the mind of the man pressed to
the limit. "Why the hell didn't you bury the body in the

Crater? Why the hell did you leave it for plane people to see. Tell me! Tell me! Tell me!"

The voice appeared to flow out through window and doorway. Captain stood to look down at Bony with eyes again masked, and on his face resignation to make Bony momentarily underestimate him.

"All right, Inspector. I'll show you," he said and turned back to a shelf above Bony's level of vision. He reached and took from the shelf a notebook, and his other hand lifted from the shelf a rifle. The notebook was dropped to the floor. The rifle was held by one hand, a finger on the trigger. Captain backed to the far end of the shelf, and the free hand reached for a cloth and small tin of oil.

Bony sat still and gazed into the orifice of the rifle held rock-steady and aimed between his eyes. He said: "To shoot me would be the stupidest thing you could do."

"It will be accidental," Captain told him, placing the oil can and rag on the table. "We are talking about legends, remember. I am cleaning the gun, and it goes off. I spring to my feet in horror, knock over the oil can, so, fling the cloth to the ground, so, and rush out for help."

Came a flurry of skirts and there was Tessa. Neither man glanced at her, the one watching Bony, Bony looking into the gun barrel.

"Captain, put that rifle away," Tessa shouted. "Put it down, I tell you. You silly idiot. You ridiculous thing, you. An accident, you'll say. Are you deaf? Put that rifle away."

The rifle didn't waver. Tessa feared to move. Bony said, with extraordinary effort to speak calmly: "If you shoot me, Captain, don't forget to pour a little of the oil on the cleaning cloth."

"And don't forget I'm here, Captain. Don't you ever forget I'm here to see you do murder, and to testify against you. You fool of a man. You silly, silly boob. You . . . If you shoot you'll hang, Captain." Tessa continued to implore.

"Then I'll shoot you too," declared Captain.

"Shows how silly you are," sneered Tessa magnificently. "The rifle is a single shot. I'd be away before you could reload."

"Cunnin' bitch, eh! Well, Tessa you been asking for it," Captain said, and, beginning to breathe hard, the barrel wavered slightly although his eyes did not. "Throwing yourself around. Making love to Old Ted. Looking on me as dirt, and on Gup-Gup and the rest. Telling the Inspector this and that, against me, against your own Tribe. Yes, Tessa, you've been asking for it, and I'm going to deal it out." Rage filled the dark eyes, twisted the face into frightening distortion. "I'm going to beat you and beat you, Tessa, as no lubra was ever beaten by her man. Yes, Tessa, you snobbish little bitch."

Captain flung the rifle behind him. It exploded the cartridge. Tessa turned about and fled through the doorway. Shouting threats, the aborigine lurched after her.

22

A MOTHER'S ADVICE

Tessa was terrified by this unsuspected Captain before whom she fled. Hitherto gentle and understanding and respectful, he was become akin to that which walks by night, the Kurdatia Man stalking young men and lubras venturing from the camp.

To gain the sanctuary of her room was the directing impulse behind the vivid picture of man in his most savage mood. She raced from the hut over the clear ground to the compound gate, and then saw standing squarely in the entrance the massive and angry form of Mister Lamb. She realised she would never by-pass Mister Lamb. She realised only too well she could not vault the fence, and the delay when attempting to climb over would mean capture.

Capture! It would mean a beating, and terrible battering pain; a smothering horror of hate and rage, and memories of other lubras being beaten and man-handled crowded her from early childhood. She heard Jim Scolloti shouting, saw him outside his kitchen and waving his arms. She heard much nearer the shouted threats of Captain, glancing back she saw him less than a dozen yards behind her. And Mister Lamb was advancing as though to cut off her way of escape.

Tessa swerved and avoided Mister Lamb, and ran on past the gateway, ran on along the compound fence. She heard Mister Lamb's thudding hooves on the ground, glanced again to the rear and saw Captain racing off course, running hard toward the Creek with Mister Lamb behind him. Heaven bless Mister Lamb! Arriving at the fence enclosing the house she pulled up, dazed and uncertain where to go now, how to get into the house, and then wanted to scream because Captain was running towards her and Mister Lamb stood baffled.

Tessa ran again, ran out to the desert. The house faded into the past where there had been love and safety and order and purpose. In its place was this open, boundless world ruled by an animate fearful thing pursuing, relentless in hate, intent upon destroying all the loveliness which once had been hers.

The desert was strange to her. Terror expunged all the colours. The sparse shrubs were brilliant grey or green. The sand was a floor of coarse stones, reddish and yet soft beneath her shoes. Lucifer's Couch was become a mountain of black and white pebbles, but the colours were absent. And there were chains and ropes whirling all about her, seeking to close upon her, bind her, cling to her as though she were a fly in a spider's web.

A shoe flew from a foot. She felt crippled, tried to kick off the other, had to stop for a precious moment to pull it off, and was now spurred by hope that she would outdistance Captain. She would circle, circle round to the homestead where the men would protect her from Captain, dear old Jim and Young Col and Bony, Inspector Bonaparte the policeman.

On a long sandy patch she glanced back. Captain was fifty yards behind. His new grey gabardine trousers were flapping at the cuffs. The sun was glinting on his chest, polishing the drops of sweat to silvered blobs. His overlong black hair was raised and shimmering in the wind he was making. Tessa veered to make the circular return to the homestead.

Hope swooned, and the springing strength in her legs seeped from them, for Captain had also veered and Tessa could see he would cut her off. She changed course again, now to head for the Creek trees among which she might be able to dodge the madman, and a moment later saw that Captain was countering this maneuver, cutting her off just like the dingoes cut out a young calf from the herd.

One of the ropes touched her. She felt its threat about her legs. It was the rope of her skirt, the white pleated skirt she loved, and now it was going to hobble her, hinder her, give her up to Captain. She must rid herself of it. But no, what indeed would Rose think or say. What would the men think, say, when she got back home? With no skirt on, with only her slip and panties? If ever she did reach home again, that is. She was running still towards the Crater, running away from the homestead, not to it, and when she had tried to circle there was Captain cutting her off. Oh, the beast! The dirty black beast!

As she ran she pulled down the side zip of the skirt. She unbuttoned the waist band, loosened the band, edged the skirt down a little, and then halted, stepped from it, and ran and ran, on towards Lucifer's Couch. This was better! She felt her legs free and strong again, and now instead of swerving to avoid low bushes she leapt over them as a young doe. And yet this couldn't go on and on for ever. She was panting for breath. She must have run miles. She wasn't able to breath properly. The stupid bra was gripping her chest, slowly tightening, giving her pain at both sides.

In a sudden frenzy she ripped the blouse down the front, caught the flapping severed ends and tore it from her. The bra! She would have to stop to get it off, or almost stop and then Captain would be upon her. And, anyway, the slip would have to come off first.

A flash to the rear revealed Captain charging after her

and less than forty yards from his intended victim. Tessa
caught up the hem of the slip, and then remembered the
strength of its material. She would never tear it as she had
torn the blouse. She could not pull it up and over her head
without being momentarily blind, to trip and fall and
never get up again. Another backward look, revealed Captain a little closer. She could see the fiendish light of
madness in his eyes, the white teeth bared in a grin of an-
ticipatory victory. And in that moment Captain failed to
see the low sand mound about the root of a once-flourish-
ing old man saltbush, and sprawled forward to skitter
along the ground, raising a low cloudlet of dust.

Tessa stopped. She heard Captain shout. She tore the
slip up and over her head. She straightened her aching
back, narrowed her shoulders, panted and cried out, managed to unhook the bra, whirl it from her arms and run
and run.

Oh, the relief, the freedom gained! Her lungs could now
expand and take in the glorious air. The pain diminished.
Her legs were like bottles, and new strength like Kurt's
sherry poured into them. The impact of the air was cool
against her breasts, her arms, her body. She knew she had
regained what they said was second wind, and another
glance behind showed her Captain was losing the race.

Now she would circle to head back home. She turned
to the south, and Captain also turned. Despair flooded
into her mind, and then hope banished despair and she
turned again to Lucifer's Couch, now no higher, looking
no nearer than she had so often seen it from the verandah.

Was she going to escape? The doubt was a flame sting-
ing her feet, her poor feet softened by years of wearing
white women's shoes. Captain's feet wouldn't be burning
like this, for he didn't wear boots or shoes unless for special
occasions. He didn't wear shoes even when he played tennis. His feet would be hard. His feet would carry him

for miles and miles until at last they caught up with her.

What could she do! For years she had lived softly on white women's tucker. Why, it must be a full year since she had chased, or had been chased, by the children in play. No one had played tennis for months. A sharp pain pierced her side and caught at her chest as the fingers of the man would soon clutch at her flesh. She gasped and cried out, faltered. The pain vanished, and she ran on, and the fear grew like a horrible old baobab tree to imprison her as the old lubra and the children had been imprisoned in Bony's legend. The real children, the tennis court, Rose and Kurt, the clothes she had worn for so long, the books and the study, the ambition to become a teacher, it hadn't been real after all. It was all a story told her by someone. Of course it was! She was an aborigine, like her mother, like Captain and Gup-Gup. The camp was real, not the white-feller homestead. Mrs. Brentner was always nice, always kind. She had taken her through the house several times, and she had often dreamed of sleeping in a room, and eating at the table, and wearing clothes like Mrs. Brentner, like Mrs. Leroy, and the other white women.

It was growing dark, and that was strange. Or had she been running from Captain for hours and hours. Must have been for hours because she was so tired she couldn't run much longer. The wind was singing in her ears, singing against the buzzing and the pounding, and in the singing she heard her mother's voice, and the voices of all the women in the world.

"Now you know what to do if you are caught away from camp by a strange aborigine," they said.

Then she heard Captain shout: "Pull up, Tessa! You can't get away from me."

"Now you know what to do—what to do—what to do."

She looked with blurred eyes for a place, a soft and

dusty place. Her hand involuntarily pressed against her hip, and she remembered she was still wearing the beautiful green silk panties. Captain shouted again, the sound was loud and close. She saw him only a little distance behind her, and she faltered to a halt. She slipped the panties from her and faced him. He shouted again, victoriously.

"What to do—what to do—what to do."

Tessa obeyed the command given by women to their maiden daughters down from the Alchuringa times. She collapsed upon the sandy ground and clawed the sand over her breasts and between her thighs. Sand fell into her open mouth, fell against the lids of her closed eyes. She heard the thud of Captain's body beside her, heard his rasping breath, heard him say: "I meant to kill you, Tessa. I meant to kill you. I don't mean to now."

The sound of their panting waned, and Tessa wanted to faint to escape the terror which returned. She saw Captain kneeling at her side, his head bowed, sweat running down his chest. She felt the gritting of the sand on her skin, and when he killed her she'd know she had beaten him of his intent. Well, why didn't he kill her? Perhaps he wouldn't after all. He was like he had always been. There was no anger, no frightened rage in his eyes and on his face, and when he spoke his voice was steady.

"You've known for a long time, Tessa, that you belong to me, not to Old Ted. You belong to the Tribe, not to Missus. You have always been my lubra. I've always cried for you, and you have always cried for me but you didn't hear. I love you, Tessa, and Missus and Kurt and Bony, and the Tribe, are not going to take you from me. We go far away, you and me. You're my woman, I am your man. Now get up and let's start."

Tessa was hauled to her feet. Her hand was gripped by his, and she was urged to walk. Her feet burned, and she limped. She felt unutterably tired and inexpressibly dirty. Her hair had lost the jewelled brooch and was full of sand. She faltered, but the vice about her hand led her on and on. A little while, and hope flared for Captain was taking her back to the homestead.

"You look a sight, Tessa," she heard him say. "You want a bath. You needn't have worked that age-old women's trick with me because us men have a trick or two to counter it."

The sun was lowering himself to rest on the Creek trees when they drew near the compound fence. Tessa was thankful that Young Col was nowhere to be seen. Old Scolloti was in the kitchen doorway, and Inspector Bonaparte was up on the tank stands. She wondered why he was there, why he didn't come down and take her from Captain. Then she saw Young Col and Mister Lamb. They were outside the carpenter's shop, and Mister Lamb was chewing tobacco.

"I can't go on, Captain," she cried. "My feet are raw. Let me go in round the back."

Captain laughed, softly, and there was no hint of sadism in the sound, no hint of anger. It sounded as though he were happy, very happy. He stopped to swing her up into his arms, and throw her over a shoulder. He laughed again and with his free hand tickled her ribs. The homestead was passing away from them, and then she realised he was carrying her to the Creek. Now his back was to the house and the carpenter's shop, and over his shoulder she was able to see Young Col urging Mister Lamb forward, aiming him.

Her abductor stopped at last, and she could see the Creek bank on either side of her. She wondered at the strength of the arm holding her upon the shoulder, wondered what was passing from his flesh to her body, a strangely ecstatic feeling.

Mister Lamb was trotting towards them. He approached with head slightly lowered from normal. Captain said: "Tessa, before I bathe you, I tell you again you are my woman because I love you."

Tessa wriggled down into the arm. Her right arm passed over his head to clamp his neck. She twisted her face and brought her mouth against his ear. She watched the advance of Mister Lamb. She giggled, and the finger of the hand about Captain's neck played a tattoo upon his powerful shoulder. When Mister Lamb was really launched she giggled again.

Then both of them were flying through the air over the water, and Mister Lamb, having been so determined, was unable not to follow them.

23

THE SITUATION IS FLUID

When Bony emerged from Captain's hut it was to see Mister Lamb determinedly charging after Captain, and beyond Captain the fleeing figure of Tessa. He was gravely perturbed by these contretemps, for Captain's reactions had been unorthodox even in an aborigine and he himself was now powerless as the riding horses had been freed into the horse paddock. He feared for Tessa because an enraged aborigine is unpredictable and as dangerous as a tiger, and he was seeking reasons for self blame as he climbed the iron ladder to the platform supporting the reservoir tanks.

At this elevation he could observe the desert beyond the house, a green speckled light-red carpet having a deep yellow fringe under the horizon sky. He was conscious of Young Col shouting up at him, and of Jim Scolloti hurrying from his kitchen with a rifle. He saw but gave no attention to Mister Lamb who was standing and staring at the departing figures.

Tessa was running well ahead of Captain. He watched her attempt to circle to the south and back to the homestead, and he saw Captain frustrate it. He saw Tessa pause to discard her shoe, and then to discard her skirt. He saw the flutter of blue and knew it was the discarded blouse, and applauded silently when she freed her body of the bra. She now had the slim grace of the deer seeking escape from the chasing hound, and for the first time he favored her. The shadows cast by the Creek trees were spreading fast across the ground below, were flowing out into the desert, making of the sunlit land a glowing garden seen from behind the bars of a prison cell. This phenomenon had but secondary importance for Bony, merely imping-ing upon his mind the fact that soon it would be dark, and darkness would advantage Tessa if only she could keep ahead of her pursuer. That she was running toward the distant golden bar of Lucifer's Couch held no signifi-cance. He could see her painted black upon the red ground, and she was divided midway by the green panties she was still wearing.

Captain was gaining steadily, and Bony came to accept the inevitable with emotions of fear over-laying frustrated anger when Tessa stopped, and her actions told of step-ping from the panties. And then she was down on the ground and the sunlight made golden the mist of sand she was clawing over herself.

"Is the bastard killing her?" shouted Young Col when standing beside him.

"It looks like it," replied Bony. "Wait, not at the mo-ment. He's kneeling beside her, and I think he hasn't touched her."

"What a ruddy mess, Bony. What happened to send Captain dilly?"

"Later, Col. Watch!"

They saw Captain stand and haul Tessa to her feet.

"Hang it, he's bringing her home," Col continued to shout. "I'll go down for the rifle."

"Bring it to me, fast," ordered Bony, adding when Col looked to question: "I said fast, Col."

Young Col brought up the rifle, and was told to secure Mister Lamb and hold him in readiness to aim at Captain should it be feasible. Delighted to do this, Young Col descended the iron ladder like a fireman, and Bony continued to observe the couple approaching the homestead.

He was immensely relieved that so far there hadn't been a violence, and, knowing aborigine psychology, dared to hope that Captain's rage had subsided, that now he was repentant and was returning Tessa to the homestead. However, when Captain swerved toward the dam, Bony understood the significance of the golden mist over the recumbent Tessa, and knew, too, the counter Captain intended to take.

Young Col was standing with Mister Lamb by the carpenter's shop, and Young Col was lost in fascinated admiration of the picture Tessa was making, until the cook yelled and the young man glanced up at Bony. Bony motioned to aim Mister Lamb, and Col bestrode him in the time-honoured fashion to direct him. Bony despaired, believing it to be too late for Mister Lamb to make contact. He could see Tessa preparing to take the shock by forcing herself lower on Captain's shoulder. Then he heard Tessa giggling, and saw her nibbling affectionately at Captain's ear. He found no humour in the sight of Captain and Tessa flung out from the bank and over the water, with Mister Lamb, unable to check momentum, following after.

Captain and Tessa arose from the depths and swam side by side up the Creek to the shallows and the sloping banks. Aborigines appeared, and Jim Scolloti yelled and shouted at them. Two dived into the Creek and swam to steer Mister Lamb to the shallows before he drowned. Others followed Captain and Tessa and ultimately gathered about them when they left the Creek. From the crowd Captain and Tessa emerged to run from the homestead again, run with apparently unimpaired strength when a white man and woman would have been exhausted.

No longer fearful for Tessa, Bony watched them. They

were running freely, for Captain now did not hold Tessa captive. They were running not fast, but together, and Bony thrilled knowing that Tessa had surrendered to the elfin call of her people, had put from her the slowly built influences of white assimilation, even as she had discarded the white women's clothes.

They dwindled to tiny dolls, animated on a cloth of gold speckled with black. The last of the sunlight created about each an aura having rainbow tints, and a moment or two later they appeared to ascend and vanish into the indigo sky at the world's end.

Bony climbed down the ladder into a world of commotion. The aborigines were clustered into groups, shouting and gesticulating. Jim Scolloti was shouting at everyone as he led Mister Lamb with a halter rope to rub him down. Young Col with hair awry and eyes clear and hard said: "So that seems to be that."

"Think you could get one of the bucks to bring in the horses?" Bony asked. "May want them first thing in the morning."

"Can do. The Brentners'll have to know of this, Bony, me lad. Rose will throw a seven, and Old Ted will be gunning after Captain."

"The situation demands calm thinking. Have the horses brought in before it's too dark." Bony's eyes grew big, and Col never forgot them. "And you keep away from the transceiver."

He entered Captain's hut. Picking up the rifle, he laid it on the table and against it placed notebooks and a wad of manuscript found in a drawer. He added several bound books after cursory examination. He switched on the electric light, thinking of the Brentners' generosity to Captain, as, too, of their generosity to Tessa, and presently found under the bed mattress another notebook, the second ivory Buddha, and a wallet.

On turning off the light, he found it almost dark, and he carried the "loot" to the office and placed it in one of the steel cabinets. Young Col, who had followed him, said: "Where do we go from here, Bony? I heard the horses being brought in." Bony asked if three or four could be fed for the night and the others turned out again, and Col said that could be done and went off to arrange it. Bony slipped the rifle behind the cabinet and went out to interview the cook.

"Don't bother about feeding us in the house, Jim. We'll eat here tonight."

"All right, Inspector. Dinner's mucked up a bit. I been attending to Mister Lamb. Had to dry him out somewhat. Now wasn't that a to-do! Cripes, it was a sight I'll never forget. As for Captain and Tessa, wait till the Boss gets home. He'll roar and scream and jump up and never come down no more."

"These things sometimes happen, Jim," Bony calmly assured him.

"You're telling me, as the American Sergeant used to say over at the Dump."

After dinner, Bony took Young Col to the office.

"I could be wrong, Col, but when Tessa and Captain came from the dam she went willingly," he said, bringing the notebooks and the rifle to the table. "What has happened to Tessa you will probably not clearly understand, the aborigines being closer to nature than the white man. There is much about Captain and his behaviour I don't understand, but I must have time to find light in the darkness."

"We should report it to the Brentners," Col said flatly.

"Not yet. Not until the situation has been resolved. Captain may bring Tessa back sometime tonight, or early tomorrow. Meanwhile I want you to collect all the guns about the place, beginning with this one, and hide them."

"From Captain?"

"And from Old Ted."

On returning to the office, Young Col found Bony studying the wall map, and they discussed the station wells and the types of power pumps used.

"Tune in the radio, please, and contact the Police Station," Bony requested, turning away from the map. His hair was dishevelled. His voice was sharp, and both his hands and walk betrayed tension. When Howard spoke, he hastened to join Young Col at the bench.

"Bonaparte here, Howard. I want you to leave first thing tomorrow with your trackers. Young Col will have a note for you if I am not here. Certain developments call for your assistance. The Brentners still in town?"

"At the dance. I told Brentner I'd take any message from Deep Creek."

"Then say all is in order, but you leave at daybreak. Clear?"

"Quite. Brentner told me they'd be heading for home about noon tomorrow. Staying on to farewell the Minister. Been a real do for Hall's Creek."

"So far good," Bony said. "Inform no one about leaving. It concerns no one."

Young Col looked with amazement at Bony, and Bony switched off the transceiver.

"Crikey! It concerns the Brentners, Bony."

"Yes, but not the general public at their transceivers," argued Bony. "Not yet, anyway. Now listen. I was talking with Captain about certain results of my investigation when suddenly he produced a rifle. Tessa appeared and dressed him down, and he flew into a rage, tossed the rifle aside and rushed at her. You saw his chase after her. I expected a killing. I know what happened to stop the threat. You saw them return to the dam into which Captain would have taken Tessa if Mister Lamb hadn't been forward. You saw them emerge and run off into the desert, and we agree that Tessa then appeared not an unwilling captive. You will agree that, other than threatening me with a rifle, Captain hasn't committed a crime. Millions of young men have chased millions of young women since Adam and Eve were banished from Eden by the front door and an original Captain and Tessa stole into Eden by the back door. Clear?"

"As sand in your eye," replied Young Col. "But when Kurt and Mrs. Brentner get home . . ." Col broke off and whistled.

"Before they arrive home Captain might have brought Tessa back," Bony pointed out. "I think it probable they will both return by breakfast time. They may return much sooner. Or they might keep going under the stars for a few hours and continue going at daylight. As the military gentlemen say, the position is fluid."

"Fluid all right, Bony. By the way they were travelling when I saw them they were headed for Paradise Rocks. Sixty-five miles and no water between. Captain will hole up with Maundin's wild blacks. I'm betting on it. He won't have the gall to face the Brentners."

"I'm inclined to bet on it too."

"You told Howard you mightn't be here when he comes. What's your plan?"

"I'll leave just before daybreak. I'll want the best horse. Think you could have it ready? I'll have to write a report for Howard, and I'll want more information from you."

"You wouldn't go alone? You'll wait for Howard and his trackers? Damn it, the wild blacks don't play ring-a-roses. They play hard."

"Let us say there's been an explosion at Deep Creek, with bits and pieces all over the station," Bony said, again calm and outwardly confident. "We must try to salvage what we can."

Yet again Bony studied the map, having motioned Young Col to join him. They discussed the outlying waters for cattle, the possible natural rock-hole waters known to Young Col, distances, and general typography coming within the limits of Col's knowledge. Admitting the possibility of Captain returning voluntarily with Tessa, he planned on the probability that Captain would defy the law.

He sent Young Col to Jim Scolloti to obtain meat and bread, tea and sugar and, from the store, a few plugs of tobacco. At ten o'clock he walked to the camp and had a man rouse out Gup-Gup and Poppa and for an hour he squatted with them over the former's little fire. On leaving them he had gained consent to perform certain acts at sunrise.

Young Col was asleep in a lounge chair in the office, and he let him sleep while he read Captain's notebooks and wrote a letter for Constable Howard and another to Rose Brentner. Young Col was still sleeping when he left the house and mounted the horse and rode out into the desert when the eastern sky was flagging the new day and the meteors were flaming over Lucifer's Couch.

24

BONY GAMBLES

The day came, and Bony was standing beside a powerful roan gelding at the place where Captain and Tessa were last seen. There were their footprints on the yielding sand. Backward, they extended down a gentle slope till lost in the sparse foot-high bush covering the northern hem of the desert. Forward, they proceeded down an opposite slope, extending into the general plain having no limits, no landmarks.

He had compelled the horse to walk all the way from the homestead to arrive here at this time, thereby conserving the animal's strength and bringing himself to the beginning of tracking the runaways at the first moment when able to see their tracks. Distance from the homestead was approximately three miles, and now mounted he permitted the horse to proceed in an easy canter and gave himself entirely to the task of reading tracks.

Certain facts had to be taken into consideration. The girl would be the weaker partner. She had led a sheltered and far from a strenuous life. She had become used to wearing shoes. She had run an exhausting race before taking this escape journey with Captain. She had run and walked three miles from the homestead to the top of this low ground swell just before darkness fell, and she was still running and walking when she made the tracks now being followed by Bony. Bony conceded it a wonderful effort.

As yet there were no highlight and shadow. The land was uniformly dun in colour, seemingly covered by a sheet of steel freezing it into changeless eternity. The sparse, low, and brittle bushes had ceased to grow a million years before, and would be so placed a million years hence. It was not last night Captain and Tessa left their tracks here in the dark: it had been when the world was being formed. Unlike the magic of the evening, the light of the dawning is often repellent.

Until the sun flashed above the horizon when the mica specks blazed with white and silver and amber lights, the bush quivered and warmed with breath, even the sand grains shivered and, if one listened, sang as the new heat warmed them.

There had been two sets of prints, and now there were but one set, the prints of the man. The girl had reached the end of her endurance, and the man had gone on with her over a shoulder. The single set of prints flowed to the south, on and on over the light sand covering the harder base, and presently there rose from the general flatness a long ridge of reddish sand, and on coming to it, Bony found it less than five feet in height, wind-carved and clean of herbage.

On the far side the man's tracks ended at a jumble of prints, his own and those made by Tessa. Here the sand was disturbed and told a story. It began about midnight when the air was cold. The man was wearing only trousers, but the woman was nude. As their wild ancestors did, they scooped a hole, laid themselves in it, scooped the displaced sand over themselves until only their faces were free. In this comparatively warm bed they had rested.

Beyond the ridge running east-west was another and beyond that doubtless others, waves of sand separated in

the troughs by narrow strips of claypan. Bony could see
the twin tracks marking the next sand slope, and from
that the tracks mounting the next. He felt confident that
Captain had left with Tessa to pass over these ridges before day broke, and what he expected happened when he
rode down the last of them to the verge of a sea of tussock
grass, grey and dead and yet resilient. Even for the experienced, this grass registered no footprints.

The shore of this sea was a ribbon of white claypan,
twelve yards wide and cement hard. The grass extended
to the west as far as could be seen, but to the south merely
a mile, and this same distance to the east. Nothing moved
upon it, and nothing less than a wild dog could be distin-
guished on the grey sheet. If Captain and Tessa had
crossed, they must have done so before he, Bony, rode
down to the shore.

On the far side, he dismounted on the claypan and
rolled a cigarette. Now looking back to the north, he saw
the smoke signals being sent up at Gup-Gup's orders.
There were three placed at equidistance: one unbroken,
one broken repeatedly, and the other less often. The homestead could not be seen, and the Kimberley mountains appeared as grey and brown rock-bars along the horizon. He
estimated his position as being about fourteen miles south
of Deep Creek, and this would place him slightly more
than fifty miles from Paradise Rocks.

According to Young Col there was no water north of
Paradise Rocks at this time, but then Young Col wouldn't
know the aborigines' secret waters so jealously protected.
Captain would instinctively locate them, and as it was by
no reasoning essential for him to proceed to Paradise
Rocks, he and Tessa could have crossed the sea of grass
in any direction to throw off probable police pursuit.
What would surely unbalance Captain's intentions was
Gup-Gup's signals calling on the wild blacks to capture

them and return them to Deep Creek Camp, and he would doubtless be dismayed and believe himself to be trapped and betrayed. The time element would depend upon the distance between himself and Maundin's tribe.

At no point had Captain paused in their flight to erase their footprints. He would be familiar with this section of country, would know that on reaching it he could thwart his pursuers by crossing the grass, or by following the claypan edging it in either direction. The grass had been eaten short by cattle, leaving the tough residue like small bunches of bristles on a wire brush. It would not deter a man having Captain's hardened feet, but would be impossible for Tessa who would have had to be carried across it. The alternative was to follow the claypan on which an elephant would not make a mark.

Bony went over in mind the conference with Gup-Gup late the previous evening. He had offered to trade, and Gup-Gup had agreed. Although the Chief had volunteered very little, by questioning Bony had learned that the wild aborigines would be following an annual timetable on walkabout to visit their secret places. This timetable would be governed by the season, and was known to Gup-Gup who said that Maundin and his people would now be holding a corroboree in camp some ninety miles to the south-west. The Chief said Captain would know this, and, on seeing the smoke signals, he would surely make for Paradise Rocks to the south-east.

Bony rode the claypan strip round the eastern end of the grass, and came to the faint motor track from the homestead to Paradise Rocks. The desert now offered vast spaces of long rises and falls, the slopes often imperceptible, the horizon seemingly distant a hundred miles, or seemingly not more than one.

There were no tracks on the motor mark spanning the desert, and Bony felt no frustration by their absence, being confident that Captain would not delay by attempting to erase their tracks. He was being forced to Paradise Rocks, and he had two burdens to carry: the knowledge that his grandfather was opposed to his flight, and a woman softened by civilisation and lacking the powers of endurance normal in an aborigine girl of her age.

Paradise Rocks, and then what? Beyond Paradise Rocks there was nothing for Captain bar thirst and starvation, and he would be forced to turn west and be caught by Maundin's bucks, and be taken back to his own camp. Bony anticipated this would be Captain's thought, and he hoped Captain would realise the situation and return to the homestead with Tessa, hoped but yet was not confident. Without a weapon of any kind, Captain could not kill a bird or animal for which the water at Paradise Rocks would be a magnet.

Therefore, he would not be surprised to see Captain and the girl coming to meet him as he rode at an easy pace toward Paradise Rocks. Neither would he be surprised if Captain lay concealed, permitting him to pass on, and then retreat to the camp at Deep Creek.

Early in the afternoon he cut their tracks when riding wide of the motor trail. The human tracks proved the fugitives were still ahead, and that Tessa was still walking. Time and distance gave assurance that they could not be very far ahead.

Towards noon the mirages became bothersome, ever threatening to deceive, offering concealment, and the light blazing upward from the sand-polished gibber fields hurt the eyes. There was no life to distract the mind, to give balance to reality. When Bony came to a wide area of sparse saltbush dotted by the stumps of swamp gums killed and blackened by fire, he found relief from what had become intolerable isolation.

The tree stumps were of all sizes and of varied height.

They were of all shapes and posture, for some of them leaned ready to be felled by the next windstorm, and against many dead buckbush lay thickly to make them appear as columns of straw. Two stumps aroused Bony's suspicions.

They were close together and presented an anomaly as elsewhere the trees had grown widely apart. One was upright, the other leaning away and seemingly ready to fall under the pressure of the next wind. They were a hundred-odd yards off the trail.

Bony rode on, the picture of a horseman anxious to arrive at Paradise Rocks and water. His suspicious eyes, however, returned again and again to these stumps. The upright one still supported a fire-blackened branch, and against the top of the partially fallen stump a mass of buckbush was trapped.

Their juxtaposition created a flaw in this picture of arid desolation, and Bony turned his horse off the trail to investigate. A waste of time, perhaps. He reined back the horse and sat staring at the stumps, and then felt a trifle foolish. Nature never creates a uniform pattern.

Dismounting, he neck-roped the horse to a stump, and withdrew the rifle from the scabbard. Keeping the weapon aimed at the upright stump, he advanced and still felt foolish yet determined to clear his mind of suspicion. They were perfect until he was fifteen yards from them, when the upright stump shivered, lost rigidity. The branch fell. The stump seemed to twist, and the top took on the profile of a man. Then Captain was standing with hands to hips and feet on their toes. The other stump slowly collapsed and lay still.

"What d'you think you are going to do, Inspector," Captain shouted derisively.

"Pump a bullet into your right leg if you don't do as you are told," Bony called back. "I have water, and tucker, and a present for Tessa. You will follow me to the horse."

Bony backed to the horse, and Captain advanced. Holding the rifle steadily upon him, Bony with his free hand unstrapped a bundle from the saddle, and beckoned Captain to draw closer. Having tossed the bundle for Captain to catch, he said: "Take them to Tessa. She will need them."

Captain obeyed, and Bony watched the fallen stump stand up, and with her back to them, Tessa proceeded to put on the skirt and blouse, and then the shoes Bony had brought for her, having in mind clear purpose. He had seen the girl fleeing from her pursuer, he had watched her discard first her shoes and lastly her panties, and he knew that during this process by degrees she relapsed into the near-primitive woman. He calculated that now as she dressed in clothes she had been educated to wear with distinction, the primitive woman would be conquered by the sophisticated girl of the homestead.

Using his feet, Bony bunched debris into a heap which he fired and added sticks. He unstrapped the quart pot and filled it from the canvas water bag slung from the horse's neck, set it to the fire and shouted: "Come on over and have a drink of tea."

Tessa came limping and obviously exceedingly tired, but Captain declined the invitation. Her hair was dishevelled. Her face bore the marks of dust and perspiration. Her eyes were wide, and rimmed with dust. Without the foundations, the smartly cut skirt and the light blue blouse made her pathetic. Bony poured water on a handkerchief, and she came to the verge of crying when wiping her face clean. From the tunic pocket he produced a comb, gave it to her with an encouraging smile.

"It's going to be all right, Tessa," he told her. "Now we have to persuade Captain to wait with us for Constable

Howard. Meanwhile, a meal and tea laced with sugar. I'll get it. You call Captain."

It was now twenty-four hours since the girl had been carried into the dam, when she may have swallowed a little water, and Bony had purposely refrained from offering her a drink from the bag. Instead of calling she went to Captain, and Bony could see argument between them, the girl pleading, the man glowering. He dropped tea into the quart pot, removed it from the fire, and having waited a full minute, divided the contents by filling the cup cap. Then he shouted again: "What's the matter? Come and have a drink of tea."

Tessa snatched at Captain's hand and began pulling him toward the waiting Bony. After stubborn refusal, Captain reluctantly permitted himself to be led, and Bony opened the parcel of food. He was on his knees when they stood at his back.

"Here it is," he said. "The pannikin for the lady: the pot for the gentleman. Sugar on offer. Spoon waiting. You must both be famished."

Not speaking, Tessa squatted on her heels, at once correcting herself by sitting on the ground and tucking her knees under the skirt. Without looking at Bony she accepted the pannikin of tea and eagerly began sipping. Beside her, Captain squatted, and fell to drinking the scalding brew. And presently they were eating and Bony was rolling a cigarette.

When finished, Captain removed from his trouser's pocket a plug of tobacco, papers, and matches. He gazed at the papers a moment before tossing them into the fire, being useless by immersion in the dam. Bony offered cut tobacco and papers, and when smoking Captain said: "Where do we go from here?"

"Back to the homestead," replied Bony. "You saw Gup-Gup's signals?"

"Must be getting wonky," Captain said, regarding Bony with shuttered eyes. "So must you, Inspector. I see you've put the rifle back into the saddle scabbard, and I'm sure I can take you any time I want to. The rifle is what we badly need. You aren't going to arrest me, so get that from your mind."

"Arrest you? I seldom make an arrest. Haven't arrested anyone for years. I leave the policemen to that. In the circumstances, it will not be I, but Constable Howard or Maundin's bucks. Late last night I talked with Gup-Gup, knowing the truth of all this business from your papers, and we reached a sensible understanding. Basically it amounts to this. The Tribe is kept out of the mess, and you take the chance of going to gaol for a few years. I say chance because I am far from certain the authorities will decide to send you there. I shall do my best to prevent it."

The shutters were raised to permit hope to flame in the dark eyes. Bony continued.

"I was sent to find out how that white man came this far into the Kimberleys without having been reported, and also what he was doing. The people who sent me are not interested in who killed him. However, the West Australian Police are interested, and it is up to them to arrest the killer. I think your worst problem is how to square with the Brentners for abducting Tessa."

For a long moment Captain studied Bony. He looked at the girl who was maintaining her gaze on the spiralling smoke of the dying fire. Wordlessly, he asked for tobacco and was rolling a cigarette when Tessa raised her eyes and spoke.

"I wasn't abducted, Bony. I ran with him. Instead of beating me into submission, he said he loved me. When he took my hand, instead of detesting him I knew I loved him. We ran together into Eden by the back door."

Tessa smiled at the still glowering Captain, and the

weariness vanished from her face. Bony looked away, feeling he had no right to share with Captain that which lived in her eyes.

"It simplifies a confused situation," he said. "Now we can persuade Constable Howard to marry you. I can see his dust too."

They stood to observe the dust cloud behind the black dot approaching like the flint head of a spear, the westering sun blood-red behind the dust. Captain gripped Bony by the arm, saying: "I'll give up if Tessa says so."

"Of course I say so," snapped Tessa, and then giggled. "You forced yourself on me, remember. Now you'll have to marry me."

Captain released Bony's arm and took Tessa's hand, and they waited silently for Constable Howard and his trackers.

25

ASSIGNMENT COMPLETED

Bony's instructions, plus pleas, in the letters he had left for Howard and the Brentners achieved an unspectacular home-coming for the fugitives. There was no one at the compound gate when the jeep arrived. The children were not in evidence. Mister Lamb was tethered to a bean tree. No aborigine lurked about the out-buildings. The only person to be seen was Rose Brentner, standing on the side verandah. And at this moment Jim Scolloti played his dinner tune on the kitchen triangle.

"Captain, I am expecting you to be your age," Bony said. "Clean yourself up and after dinner wait in your hut till called." He took Tessa by the arm. "Tessa, come with me and keep your feet from shuffling."

Tessa expected banishment to the camp, and as she was led to the verandah Bony could feel her trembling and through his fingers sent a message of comfort. Rose was calm, and a segment of history was repeated when she took Tessa's hand and led her off to the bathroom "to be scrubbed down."

There was no time to change for dinner at which neither Tessa nor the little girls were present. It was eaten in almost complete silence, Kurt Brentner wanting to know what had been done with the horse and being told by Howard that one of his trackers was riding it back. Afterwards, he accompanied the policeman and Bony to his office, a large man when set with them.

"How far out did you get 'em?" he said demandingly.

"About forty miles. They were making for Paradise Rocks. Tessa was all in, and I think Captain had had enough. There was no difficulty."

"Beats me," declared Brentner. "Not normal for Captain go run amok like that, or for Tessa to run away with him, willingly, so Jim and Young Col say. We've done everything for both." His voice became a whip. "What happened. What in hell happened?"

Bony's eyes abruptly blazed.

"The most wonderful thing on earth when, during great stress, a young man and a young woman realise they are in love. It is quite a story, and I want them both to be present, together with your wife. Will you call Captain, please?"

Brentner strode from the room, grim and purposeful, and now Howard regarded Bony quizzingly, his eyes small, his mouth tight.

"This affair has queer angles," Bony told him. "Decisions will have to be made by the Top Brass, yours and mine, and it might be unwise for us to act together or alone. At this particular moment, I can say that motives behind the Crater crime are not really bad."

"You have tidied it up, then?"

"Yes, Howard, I've done that. I am hoping to leave with you tonight to board the early plane tomorrow. I feel sure you will agree that when I've done with these people neither of us should stick out his neck."

Rose entered with Tessa, and he was saying he would be leaving later this evening and then asking if he might bid good-bye to the children, when Brentner came in with Captain.

"Now that we are all here," Bony said when they were seated as he directed, "I am going to urge you to be very frank and truthful not only for your own sakes but for others. My investigation into the death of a man hasn't been very difficult, and was actually assisted by Captain's flair for writing history. I was able to avail myself of his records rather soon than late because of that rough temper he has and which he must learn to keep under control."

Captain looked up from gazing at his immaculate tennis shoes to concentrate on Bony. His face bore no expression.

"It is known that the Indonesians claim Dutch New Guinea as part of their Empire, and it is also known that subversion and infiltration has been going on in that part of New Guinea.

"These Asians are confident they will eventually gain Dutch New Guinea through the Western Nations' passion for compromise or appeasement, which of course is always accepted as weakness, and that having gained this territory, they will proceed to work for the other half of the island governed by Australia. Following success there, they will demand, with grounds for hope, that the northern half of Australia will be surrendered to them. These are the views set down by Captain, who has as much right to record his opinions as any one of us.

"This time last year the Asians sent emissaries into this quarter of Australia to make contact with the aborigine tribes to prepare the way for an important agent. Their job was to promise liberation by driving the white man out and throwing open the white man's stores, thought by the great majority of aborigines to contain unlimited supplies of food and tobacco. The emblem of the mysterious liberating power was Buddha carved on ivory.

"When two of these pathfinders came to Deep Creek they were met with hostility which brought on a fight, Captain retaining the marks of this fight and Mr. Brentner noting the fact in his work diary.

"Captain is undoubtedly an intelligent man, but he revealed lack of wisdom. Had he reported the mission of these two strangers . . . noted by Mr. Brentner as aborigines . . . subsequent events might not have followed. Had Mr. Brentner dug into the cause of the fight, instead of noting it was merely an aborigine affair, the present situation might well not have arisen. It becomes clear that both Mr. Brentner and Captain were influenced by determination to maintain the status quo of this Deep Creek Tribe: the one having in mind the equitable arrangement by which he obtains stockmen when required, and the other having in mind the delaying as long as possible of assimilation of his people with a race unworthy of accepting them.

"Permit me to digress. A few years after the last war I heard a legend which goes something like this. In the days of Alchuringa a being having the head of a dingo and the body of man hunted with another having the body of a dingo and the head of a man. They had caught a black-fellow and were about to cook him on a fire when the Father of the Iguanas slid down the smoke column, puffed the fire apart, and when safely ringed by flames, said: 'The aborigine was here before you. He will be here when the white man comes on walkabout. When the white man has perished he will still be here. Then will come the brown man who will walkabout for a long time and be good friends with all the black men. There will be plenty of tucker all the time.' Having said this the Father of the Iguanas puffed the surrounding flames out upon the monsters who were burned up. He then climbed up the smoke column to the sky, and the black-fellow escaped and ran home.

"This legend came here to Deep Creek. I read it among those set down by Tessa. It is a false legend because no genuine legend contains a prediction. However, it has circulated very widely, having been passed from tribe to tribe, and it can be said that its purpose was to prepare the ground to receive the seed sown by the brown men.

"Captain, tell me how you came to have an ivory Buddha." (Captain sat up a little startled.) "It was under your bed mattress."

"One of the strangers had it round his neck," replied Captain. "I tore it off him. The one you said you saw in the Tribe's Treasure House was taken from the other by Poppa." Captain chuckled. "Those two fellers weren't worrying about the Buddhas when they left."

"They were followed by the man found dead on Lucifer's Couch," Bony continued. "Who he was I don't know, but Security identified him and for its own reasons withheld the information from me. However, Captain states in his writings that he was definitely English and probably Australian. It is also recorded that he was a remarkable linguist, an expert on aboriginal dialects, a remarkable man in other respects for he was able to travel through the most inhospitable area in all Australia without meeting opposition until he came to Deep Creek; not the main camp, but a secret camp two miles further down.

"He was an agent of a foreign government, for he, too, possessed a small ivory Buddha. What happened to him? He came with Maundin when that wild gentleman visited Gup-Gup, having been passed on to Maundin's tribe by another farther south, and it appears he didn't enter the country via a seaport as among his papers there is mention of leaving Innaminka, near the border of New South Wales, as well as the date.

"Captain was with the Elders who listened to him at the secret camp. He was enraged by the fellow's promises that soon the brown men were to come and kill the whites, open the stores, and hand out guns to shoot the cattle. Captain records that he spoke fluently in their dialect and gave evidence of thinking as the aborigine does. His work was to germinate the seed sown by the forerunners, eventually found in Derby, in ground prepared by the false legend.

"It would seem that he was accidentally killed at a send-off ceremony during which the local aborigines gave a display of boomerang throwing. Captain was not present at this boomerang throwing, but he says that the white visitor, instead of dodging a returning boomerang, ran and was struck on the head.

"Having the reputation of being a fixer, Captain was sent for. Instead of reporting the affair to the police, action which would have resulted in enquiry, grave suspicion, and possible removal of the men to the Penal Settlement, he decided to deal with the body as none knew who the man was or whence he came.

"Gup-Gup and Poppa wouldn't permit burial or destruction anywhere on their tribal ground, every inch of which being hallowed by custom and history. There was one place not important to the Tribe, and Gup-Gup and Company found no objection to the body being taken to Lucifer's Couch. The Crater was seldom visited by white men, and in case it was visited again by scientists interested in finding the remains of the meteor, and mining for it, it was planned to stage the death of a man from thirst. Such an end would account for the absence of equipment.

"Captain cut two poles, using a saw from the carpenter's shop in preference to an axe which would have been heard at the house. Wearing moccasins of hessian bagging to minimise his tracks, he conveyed the dead man by night and left him on Lucifer's Couch. That would seem to be that."

Bony proceeded to roll a cigarette, and the silence was broken by Rose Brentner.

"How were the poles used? Why poles?"

"As an ambulance stretcher," replied Bony.

"Oh! Then that would mean two men. Who was the second man?"

26

THE SECOND MAN

Bony skipped Rose Brentner's question, and addressed himself to Captain.

"On reading your account of the activities of these strangers I find support for it in the small notebook and the small Buddha hidden under your mattress; however, the story of the boomerang throwing at the farewell ceremony is at odds with the facts.

"I wonder why you kept those articles, and I wonder why you wrote about the affair at all. From the condition of the ink on the paper I shall assume that you wrote the account after I appeared and began to prod people into action. It lends further strength to the contention that the boomerang story is a fake."

Captain continued to sit easily in his chair. His face bore an expression of pained interest, but his eyes admitted nothing.

"Did you interfere with the transceiver when the plane reported the man in the Crater?" Bony asked.

"Yes, I did. I wanted to stop Constable Howard coming too quick. Gup-Gup ordered a walkabout, and I wanted time to convince him it would be the worst thing to do. He wouldn't listen, and then I had to get back to connect the power again before Mr. Leroy came, and I had trouble getting Tessa away from the lubras when Poppa told them to keep her."

"That fits, Captain. Now tell me why you sent Mitti to get out to Eddy's Well before Young Col and me."

"Wondered why you were going out there, that's all. I had to know everything you did." Captain crossed his legs, glanced at Tessa as though seeking admiration for astuteness.

"That business cost the Station a useful horse and much time looking for him. It was as well I was out there to observe Poppa and others cut up the horse and toss the parts into a mine shaft. You are too prone to underestimate people, Captain. You couldn't remain still. You had to move when I prodded, and keep moving. Tell me, who was the other man who helped carry the rough stretcher?"

"I'll never say," Captain vowed.

"You will so," Tessa exclaimed, adding: "Remember what Inspector Bonaparte said about it being best for everybody to tell the truth. Tell it, then."

"Telling it wouldn't make it either better or worse, so don't you start in on me." Transferring his gaze back to Bony, he continued: "I'm willing to take the blame for moving the body to the Crater. I did what I thought was best for my people."

"And I am doing what I think is the best for your people," Bony continued. "I think your story of the boomerang is so unrelated to reality that the authorities will not accept it. What say you, Howard?"

"Too far-fetched for me to digest, Inspector."

"Captain, you are like the man who was travelling south, and found himself veering to the west. When correcting the error he veered too far to the east, and so was lost. Your boomerang story inculpates all your people."

"It was an accident. It happened."

"The law won't believe anything until it gets the lot of you on the mat," Howard asserted.

"Can I ask a question?" Brentner interrupted. Bony

nodded. "Why did you go with Young Col to Eddy's Well that day. It seems that Captain's troubles began with sending Mitti out there."

"As you say, Captain's troubles really began that day, Mr. Brentner. I went with Young Col merely for the ride to see the country."

"Just shows how much of a fool you were," Brentner told Captain. "Cost the company a horse, and dragged the Tribe into this business."

"I have been a fool too," admitted Bony. "I made several mistakes, one being to accept the medical estimate of the time the man was dead. You will remember that it was from three to six days. I concentrated on those six days. I should have known better, even though I had studied the photographs taken of the body indicating it was three days, not six. I should have made due allowance for the lack of humidity in the Crater, for the man had been dead seven days when the body was discovered. He died on April 20. Incidentally that was Tessa's official birthday.

"On the afternoon of this day, Captain mended Rosie's box in the carpenter's shop, and removed a saw with which he cut the poles. It was the day, Mr. Brentner, that you drove to Laffer's Point to repair the pump. You returned late that day. What time was it when you got home?"

"Pretty late. About midnight. The track's very rough."

"You had then repaired the pump?"

"Yes. It's why I was so late getting home."

Rose Brentner was now studying her husband, and when she turned to Bony, she was smiling.

"That's right, Inspector. I remember Kurt telling me he worked on the pump until it was almost dark."

"It is not true that the pump at Laffer's Point was removed two weeks before April 20 and sent to Hall's Creek for repairs, and was not re-installed until one week after April 20."

Brentner sprang to his feet, anger blazing in his eyes. From Bony he glared at Captain, and the aborigine rose to his feet slowly, to stand with his fists dug into his hips. At this moment of strain, Bony remembered that Young Col had referred to Captain and Old Ted as pots coming to the boil, and he said: "It was not Captain who put the lid on this pot. Please be seated, Mr. Brentner. Captain may have acted foolishly, but never disloyally. You did not go to Laffer's Point that day, or did you?"

"No I didn't go out there." Brentner resumed his seat and wiped his forehead with a handkerchief. His wife was regarding him with eyes wide and unwinking. He said: "As you pointed out, Inspector, Captain is a fool but hasn't been disloyal. He slewed me about sending Mitti to Eddy's Well, or admit to the results of it. I suppose his idea was to save me from worrying, or it was to boost his ego as a fixer. Anyway, I'm man enough at this stage not to let him take all the knocks.

"First thing that day—yes, it was April 20—Captain told me about this white agitator and what he had said to Gup-Gup and the others the night before at the temporary camp. I went there with Captain. I intended to be peaceable, to get rid of him, the last thing I wanted being to prevent the Tribe being involved with subversion. I told the feller to get going. Instead of clearing out he gave me lip. I clouted him one, and he fell back and hit his head on a tree root."

"Was Maundin present?"

"No. He left for his own camp the day before. So I had a dead agitator on my hands, and that was something which couldn't be left to Captain to fix. When we said we'd take care of the body, bury it or something, the abos wouldn't

stand for it being done on their territory which didn't
rightly include the Crater. And so I sent Captain to cut
two poles while I stayed with Gup-Gup in that camp. I
talked to the aborigines, and they were with me all
through. Yes, Rose, I was the second man."

"Why did you state in the work diary that you went to
Laffer's Point? Is the diary that important?" queried Bony.

"Yes, it is important," Brentner replied. "It's this way. On
the first of every month a copy of the work done the month
before has to be sent down to the Company Office, and the
job has always been done by my wife on her typewriter."

The cattleman was now sitting crouched forward, his
hands together between his knees. Rose went to him to sit
on the arm of his chair and slip her arm about his neck.
A long silence was broken by Constable Howard.

"It's still your case, sir."

"That's so, Howard. Thank you for reminding me. I believe that is what did happen. Last night Gup-Gup went
some distance which confirms it. I am going to leave it to
the Brass. You?"

"I'm all for passing the buck."

"Mr. Brentner," Bony said softly. "Under other circumstances I would have to ask Constable Howard to take you
into custody on a charge of manslaughter, together with
several lesser charges. You may ultimately be so charged,
and I am glad to be able to pass the buck. Although your
anger was righteous, a man was killed. Personally I cannot criticise the motive you had when going to the camp,
and personally I . . . well, were I not a police officer I
think I might have acted as you and Captain did, following the accident. Have I your word that neither will leave
the homestead until higher decisions have been made?"

"Of course you have it. I think it's ruddy decent of you."
Rose stood and said: "I think so too." Mastering the

catch in her voice, she called to Tessa: "Come along and help with the supper, Tessa."

Tessa almost ran to her, and they were stopped by Bony who said: "There is a little something to be done by Constable Howard after supper. You failed to bring off a marriage, Mrs. Brentner. I shall not fail to bring off this one."